Nineteen Ninety-Four

It was a bright cold day in January, and the clocks were bleeping ten. In Bluff Cove Crescent the milkman sat in the warmth of his float and directed a wire-guided robot which zipped from door to door. At the end of the crescent stood a colossal billboard. Its surface was filled with the face of a distinguished grey-haired man, who smiled sagely above a slogan in crisp gold capitals:

THE ENVIRONMENT IS ALL
AROUND US . . .

Nineteen Ninety-Four

Robert Lindsay	Edward
Siobhán Redmond	Sophie
Paul Shearer	Charles
David Goodland	Sir Desmond
Stephen Fry	Bishop

Other parts played by

Pam Ferris
Emma Thompson
Hugh Laurie
Richard Turner
Mark Knox
Christopher Barr

Produced in Manchester for BBC Radio 4 by
Nick Symons

Nineteen Ninety-Four

WILLIAM OSBORNE & RICHARD TURNER

ARROW BOOKS

To Nick Symons

Arrow Books Limited
62–65 Chandos Place, London WC2N 4NW

An imprint of Century Hutchinson Limited

London Melbourne Sydney Auckland
Johannesburg and agencies throughout
the world

First published 1986

Photoset in Linotron Ehrhardt by
Rowland Phototypesetting Limited
Bury St Edmunds, Suffolk
Printed and bound in Great Britain by
Anchor Brendon Limited, Tiptree, Essex

ISBN 0 09 945150 6

1
WORK IS FREEDOM

It was a bright cold day in January, and the clocks were bleeping ten. In Bluff Cove Crescent the milkman sat in the warmth of his float and directed a wire-guided robot which zipped from door to door. At the end of the crescent stood a colossal billboard. Its surface was filled with the face of a distinguished grey-haired man, who smiled sagely above a slogan in crisp gold capitals:

THE ENVIRONMENT IS ALL AROUND US

Inside the bedroom of number thirty-two Edward Wilson was frowning. His alarm had woken him for no apparent reason and they had argued. Now his television was showing the news. He told it to be quiet. In his right hand he toyed with a micro diary recorder, another useless Christmas present from his grandmother, whom he hadn't seen for years. She had included four hundred blank tapes and the message in a frail and wavering voice, 'Send Nanny a note', on the one inside the machine. In the corner of his room his Fetcher yapped childishly for some attention. Edward picked up a climbing boot and hurled it. The Fetcher fell silent.

Dear Granny, he began, and stopped. He pressed the erase button and told the thermostat to warm the room up a bit. In the hall the letter flap clacked as the milkman's robot thrust a Platinum Casino Card through.

Dear Diary. Today is the fifth day of January in the year of our Lord 1994. I have decided to record a diary to set down the events of my life for you in the future. Also I have four hundred blank tapes from my grandmother. Why are old people so behind the times? Nobody keeps a diary nowadays. What's wrong with a nice pair of socks? The journal of Edward Wilson. People always talk about the weather in diaries – well, this will be a frank view of my life only, that I pledge.

Edward paused to ask the teamaker to hurry up. It flicked to Turbo Boil.

Last night to the cineplex. Wanted to see Helmut Blender's *A Girl, A Dog, A Piece of Cheese*, but it was full. Instead watched the double feature in screen 27. It was packed, and I'm not surprised. First film was a dance adventure. A group of chic teenagers meet up with a disco dance champion on the run from an evil professor of designer leisurewear. Together they invent a new style of dance and use its mystical force to thwart the professor. Audience went bonkers in the dance sequence. The main picture was a war adventure set on the planet Xerox. A bad copy of *Intergalactic Bloodbath 2*. Comma, the hero, singlehandedly massacres an entire space tribe which has unfairly beaten his own people through the cynical manipulation of public opinion. Good scene where King's head imploded with a proton mallet. After the film finished, some of the audience chanted the title, *Comma, the Full Stop* for five minutes. Got caught by the flag women on the way out.

The tea was ready. Edward poured himself a mug and sipped from it thoughtfully.

Slipped on some ice on the way home. Some people laughed. Man can be cruel. Ice can be cruel. Today it is cold. I hate cold weather, it makes everywhere so cold. Don't much like wet weather either. Tonight I shall watch telly, although decent programmes on a Monday night are still a chimera. The final of *Nicest Young Person in the Environment* is on. Will probably go to bed early.

He put the recorder down and thought about his own childhood in Berkhamsted. He remembered the Christmas holidays well, the in-laws, the sales, the influenza. In a

6

funny way he had been grateful when the Difficulties had come along. Berkhamsted hadn't.

Dear Diary, here is some personal information in case of loss. My credit number is 44987654W223, my cash number is 567773 . . .

The phone buzzed.

'That'll be the telephone,' chirruped the alarm.

'Why do you do that? Hallo?'

'Mr Wilson?'

'Yes.'

The man on the other end of the phone looked at the dishevelled, unshaven and pallid object that appeared on his screen.

'The Environment wants you for an interview at the Department at two o'clock this afternoon. Don't be late.'

'What?'

'You'd forgotten, hadn't you?'

'No, no. What time?'

'Two o'clock. You're wondering what the hell it's all about.'

'Don't be absurd.' Edward wished he would go away.

'Goodbye.'

'Wait.' For no good reason his heart was thumping. He tried to think what it could all be about. Nothing was the only answer he could come up with. The pounding in his chest slowed. Every time the Environment requested to see him he suffered that same feeling of guilt he had had after looting in the Difficulties.

'What time is it, alarm?'

'It will be 10:21 and six seconds . . . now.'

'You're such a pedant.'

'No I'm not. Can't you distinguish between pedantry and fine accuracy. I am accurate to one millisecond every . . .'

'All right, all right. How many seconds?'

'Six.'

'Gosh, six seconds, better get up, then. Naughty Edward staying in bed till now.'

He picked up the recorder.

Dear Diary, Star Date fifth of the first, 1994. Captain's Log. Have been requested to go to the 'Department of the Environment' at two o'clock for an interview I know nothing about. Suspect a trap. Will take a packed lunch.

He tossed the machine on to the bed and walked into the bathroom.

'Good morning, Edward, want a shave 'n' shower?'

'Morning bath.'

'Good morning, Edward, want a shave 'n' shower?'

'Morning.'

'Good morning, Edward, want a . . .'

Edward thumped the control panel with more than the necessary force. He stuck his tongue at the mirror and noted its jaundiced hue. He looked rather older than his twenty-seven years: thinning hair and thinning face. The door bell chimed.

'That'll be the door bell,' chirruped the alarm.

'Is it a joke? Is that why you do it?' He wrapped a robe around himself and opened the door.

'Hallo, Edward. I'm so sorry to bother you . . . I . . .' It was the woman from next door.

'Oh, Mrs . . .'

'Pearson.'

'Mrs Pearson. Something not working properly?'

'Oh, how did you guess, Edward? It's the washing machine, it's refusing to go.'

'I'll get some clothes on and come over.'

'You're an angel, Edward.'

'Yes, right, see you in a minute.'

Out of the bedroom window he watched her walk back across the crescent to her house. She must have been freezing in that leotard. She was about thirty-five but did her best to try and look much younger. She was fighting a losing battle. Edward pulled some clothes on.

'Fridge, what have we got to eat?'

'Nothing. The milk's gone off, the bread is like rock and the cheese is set to walk. When are you going to defrost me?'

'Do it yourself or I'll let the Fetcher have a go.'

'Fascist.'

He tripped the door switch and walked over to the house opposite. Through the patio doors of the Pearsons' lounge he saw the Christmas tree lit by coloured lights. Mrs Pearson was doing exercises in front of the gas log fire. He knocked on the door.

'Thank you for coming so quickly, Edward. I'm just useless when it comes to *these kind* of things.' She gripped his arm.

The Pearsons' house was bigger than Edward's. It was also cleaner, but cluttered with every gadget and appliance the Environment had to offer. Edward threaded a path through the ankle-deep sea of toys. Laser guns, light ships, space monsters and computer packs lay where they had been flung. From the playroom came the roar and screams of a frightful space game played by ghastly children.

'Children, be quiet please.' The noise rose. 'They're such funsters.' She smiled weakly.

Edward looked at the washing machine. Its control panel was flashing spasmodically.

'Hallo, washing machine. Can you hear me?' It was silent. 'How long have you had it?'

Mrs Pearson knelt close. There was an overpowering smell of perfume.

'Oh, it's practically new. Perhaps the children have been playing with it. If Colin were here he . . .'

Colin was her husband. He epitomized the image of a perfect family man one saw on advertisements. Handsome, reliable, practical, Edward remembered he had volunteered

9

for ad service just after the new year. It had been the third time in the previous six months.

'He's in the North at the moment, on low-fat margarine. Phones me every night. So dependable.'

But never here when you needed him, thought Edward, who knew absolutely nothing about the chips inside a Turbo Tumble 2001 from the planet Zonda. He fiddled with the control disks and the drum thrashed the clothing briefly and stopped.

'Have you got a spanner?'

'Why do you want a spanner?' blurted the machine.

'Oh, so we're talking, are we?' The machine didn't answer.

'I don't know.' She rested a hand on his shoulder. 'It came with this.' She handed him a flat piece of metal with various shapes cut out of it. Edward looked for somewhere to attach it to.

'Why not change into some overalls? You'll get your clothes filthy. Come upstairs and I'll show you . . .'

Edward thumped the front panel.

'I think you'll have to get the man out, Mrs Pearson.'

'It's Joanne. Why, what's the matter?'

'It's not working.'

The playroom door was flung open and two children charged into the kitchen, shouting at the top of their shrill little voices. All children were horrible nowadays, he thought.

'Freeze, space prat!' The boy screamed at Edward holding an enormous plastic gun with both hands at the end of outstretched arms. He was about eight or nine but, because of the high-protein diet he had been fed since birth, looked much older. His younger sister stood next to him, her decay-free teeth gripping the pin on some ferocious-looking grenade. Both were wearing the uniform of the Space Hawks, a force of children dedicated to stamping out senseless road accidents involving young people across the universe.

'Sebastian, Jemima, Mr Wilson is trying to fix the washing machine.'

'He couldn't fix a meteor storm even with a destructor wand!'

'Sebastian.'

'Hallo, Sebastian.'

'Shove it, anti-matter.' Sebastian jabbed the gun into Edward's ribs.

'Now look, children, please leave the grown-ups alone ...' She looked at Edward apologetically. 'It's the food colouring, I'm afraid. I've stopped all the red and yellow food, but Sebastian sneaks out and buys them those new blue snack things.'

The children were racing around the kitchen, arms outstretched, zapping everything in their cross-hairs. They aimed at their mother and she squeezed close to Edward for protection.

'Well, I'll have one last go, Mrs Pearson.'

'Joanne.'

He knelt back down with the metal instrument and tapped the glass. Two out-of-breath and smelly children crowded round.

'If Colin were here we wouldn't need this berk,' Sebastian said encouragingly.

'It's Daddy, not Colin, please.'

'It's Colin until he's earned our respect.'

'Our respect, our respect,' chanted Jemima.

Edward reset the programme but the machine didn't respond.

'We'd send you back to the planet Zonda, you piece of junk, but it got blasted by the Meltemi last week,' screamed Sebastian.

'Didn't,' cried the machine.

'Did too.'

'Didn't,' blubbed the machine.

'Did too, did too,' the children chanted.

'Didn't,' said Edward.

'Shut up, bog face,' shrieked Jemima.

'It didn't,' repeated Edward. 'Now listen, Zonda is perfectly all right, orbiting quite normally and – and you needn't take any notice of these two *androids* in future.' The machine gave a sigh and kicked back into life. Mrs Pearson's whites would turn out right after all.

'Mummy, Mummy, he called us androids.'

'There, there, have a yummy salt 'n' sugar snack.' She handed out bags to the children, who, mollified, ran screaming back into the playroom and slammed the door.

'Edward, how can I thank you? You're so mechanical, so physical.'

'Oh it's nothing, Mrs Pearson.'

'Joanne.'

'Oh, mustn't leave a job half finished.' He spotted the metal tool, retrieved it and handed it to Mrs Pearson. She toyed with it languorously.

'Stay for coffee. I'd like you to see our new sun bed and . . .'

'I can't, I'm afraid . . .'

'Afraid?'

'Afraid I've got an interview at two o'clock.' He made for the door. She opened it for him.

'My husband doesn't get back till the weekend, Edward.'

'Goodbye, Mrs Pearson.' He hurried away from the ideal family back to his house, blushing fiercely and picturing the scene he had so narrowly avoided. *That* would have made an interesting diary entry.

Edward arrived with ten minutes to spare for the interview. The Department was housed in an enormous steel and mirror-glass building running from Hyde Park to Marble Arch and stretching back into the heart of the capital. He stepped into the entrance plaza and walked to the check-in desk.

'Hallo, check-in.'

'Hi, welcome to the Environment,' said the check-in.

'I've got an interview.'

'Which department?'

'I don't know, isn't that your department? The Department of the Environment, I suppose.'

'My department? But I don't have a department. Which department of the Department of the Environment?'

'I've come for an interview.'

'You've come to the right place. We're the ones who care, the ones who share, the ones who . . .' It stopped. A message appeared on the screen. *We are sorry for this break in our programmes. Have a nice day.*

Edward found a lift, and ascended. Twenty minutes later he got out.

'Honestly, guv, it's got to be this floor. This time. I think,' the lift said. Edward spotted a young woman typing at the end of the corridor.

'Excuse me, is this where the interviews are?'

'Yes,' she shouted back.

He ran up.

'Sorry, didn't want the lift to strand me. Edward Wilson, sorry I'm late. In there, is it?' He pointed to a door.

'That's right. They'll call you in. Sit down, get your breath back. I'm Sophie.'

'I'm Edward.'

Sophie laughed raucously.

Behind the door, a man and woman sat poker-faced in front of two monitors and surveyed the mass trivia of Edward's recorded life. The reasons behind the failure of his last relationship were being displayed – misunderstood needs and unpaid phone bills. A transcript of his last visit to the dentist came up next. They sniggered. The man pressed a button.

'Send him in Miss, er, send him in.'

Edward shuffled in briskly. They registered 'arrogant swagger' on their assessment disks.

'So, Edward, tell us all about yourself.'

'There's not much to tell.'

'Oh, I don't know.'

'Well I really want . . .'

'Yes?'

'Well I wouldn't mind knowing what I'm doing here.'
There was a frosty silence.

'It's about a job, if you must know.'

'What job?'
The silence returned.

'Well, I think it's a little premature to er . . .'

'Yes, let's get the job first, shall we, and then find out.
If we knew what it was we'd do it ourselves.'

'If you'd like to wait outside, we'll call you back. We have
a few things to discuss.'

Edward got up and went to rejoin Sophie.

'How did it go in there? Tough questions?' It was an
alluring accent, which he took to be Glaswegian.

'One or two.' He looked her over. She was a cracker. Five
foot eight, thick strawberry blonde hair permed into golden
coils, and soft Celtic green eyes. But she was not a stereotype.
Her mouth was quite narrow and her nose larger than the
de rigueur retroussé ski jump. She was dressed casually, but
Edward's imagination discerned a good body underneath.
He asked her about herself. She was a single hard-working
career girl. She lived alone except for a cat called Eisenstein but
felt it very important not to become withdrawn or introverted.
She evidently enjoyed life to the full. Edward hated this vacu-
ous type of hedonist. They were as sincere as newsreaders.
But somehow . . . The buzzer went.

Inside, the man switched off the magazine he was reading.

'Well?'

'The Mainframe has given him the job,' the woman said.

'Ours not to reason why.' The door opened.

'Well, Edward, you've won it. The job is yours.'

'When do I start?'

'When you like. Come and go as you please.'

'Don't do anything rash,' said the woman. 'In fact, don't do anything. That's the best policy. Keep a low profile.'

The screen gave a bleep.

'Oh, that reminds me.' She handed him a pack of disks. 'Theological, political, medical, intimately personal, that sort of thing. Fill them out when you've got a moment.'

'Where shall I report to when I start?'

'It's all on the video,' the man reassured him.

'What video?'

'The one we've just sent you. Bye-bye.'

They pushed him out into a deserted corridor and the door swished shut. For no good reason, Edward swore.

The next morning he awoke with the same word 'Camembert' on his lips. The television was warming up.

'. . . and squeeze to the left and pull to the right and tuck that knee in till it hurts and twist the neck for all it's worth and slide your hands . . .'

'Shut up.' He looked at his watch. 'Tea, please.' Closing his eyes he tried to remember what his dream had been about but it had vanished.

'Fetcher, get me some clothes.' The machine whirred across the room, smashed into the wardrobe and lay on its side.

He looked out of the window. Some men were changing the face on the billboard to a different benign pose with the slogan:

SMILEABILITY: THAT'S THE ENVIRONMENT'S
PLEDGE

Edward renewed his new, unfashionable pastime.

6 January 1994. Dear Diary, today I go to work for the first time. Will probably resign. Last night got bored so placed a logic bomb in one of the questionnaire disks they gave me. Outside the weather continues cold. Mrs Pearson has just come out of their

sauna into the snow. She really must try to eat a little less. Now she is looking in this direction and adjusting her bikini top. I hope she gets pneumonia. Won the bingo on Channel 26 last night and will receive a basket of currency.

Seem to be losing weight in the night and gaining it again during the day. This worries me. I worry too much. The microwave has broken so the house is like a ship without a ... without a microwave.

My first impressions of work will follow.

He walked into the bathroom and took pills from a variety of bottles – Plasma Activate, Protein Generate, Multi-Complex Amino Buster – and swallowed them down. The post flap clacked.

'That will be the milkman,' chirruped the alarm.

'If that's a joke, alarm. It's getting boring.'

It was the introductory video from the Environment. He picked it up and popped it into the machine.

'Hi there, Edward Wilson. Congratulations, a job of infinite pleasure and fun awaits you. Here is a plan of the Department. You are here. Take the lift to the second floor and ...'

There was a deafening explosion followed by a roaring sound. His front windows had imploded. A shower of wood and glass filled the room. Edward lay on the carpet, his head ringing. He felt sick. Strong hands grasped him and pushed him on to the sofa. A thick-set athletic man sat on his chest.

'Help!' Edward struggled in the vice-like grip.

'Shut it,' the man rapped through a thick black balaclava. Other men, identically dressed, were ransacking the house, except for one who was spraying some smouldering curtains with a fire extinguisher. The man jumped off his chest.

'Right, fall in, men. Wait for it, wait for it ... two, three ...'

> I adore you dear,
> You know that's clear.

You hold my love hostage,
You naughty love terrorist.
Snuggles and hugs,
Birthday Boy,
Love, Simone.

They had barked it in absolute synchronization.

'Right, men, move out.'

'Just a bloody minute.'

'Yes, Mr Walker?'

'Look what you bastards have done to my house.'

'We just deliver 'em, Mr Walker. Is the plastic set?'

'Sir.'

'I'm not Mr Walker.'

'Tell that to the Marines. Let's go, go, go, go, go . . .'
The men raced from the house. Edward followed them.
Behind him the demolition charges in the kitchen went
off.

'I'm not Mr Walker, you stupid, stupid bastards.' The
half-track pulled away.

'Think yourself lucky it was only an SASagram, Mr
Walker,' the leader bellowed back.

Edward walked back up the path. Inside, the damage
was not too bad but the alarm had called the emergency
services. A siren sounded in the crescent and there was the
clump of heavy boots.

'We came as quick as we could. You all right?'

'Yes, I'm fine.'

'Pity. Can you stand just there please and hold this
broken vase and look sad. OK? Lovely. You get that,
Bill?'

'Yeh, great one. What about the old "Look at my burnt-
out kitchen" shot?'

'Yeh, OK. If you wouldn't mind, sir. Lovely. Great. So
what was it? Passionate teenage romance with kooky bride
to be? Vengeance of a scorned lover? Pranks for preppies?'

'Wrongly addressed.'

'That's novel . . . Yeh, might be something in that.' A third man joined them. His tie was awry and he smelt of alcohol.

''Ere, Nick, Bill. Got an emergency. Suspected den of vice. Come on . . .'

'See you . . . Thanks, mate.' There was a screech of tyres and the sirens wailed once more.

Edward walked into the bedroom and filled his pockets with plastic cards. Then he placed a call through to 'Double Glaze: No Pane with Us', wedged the shattered door shut and, glancing up at the billboard, set off for the tube. The eyes of the old man met his.

'Smileability, that's the Environment's Pledge,' a deep, soft, wise voice soothed from the speakers.

Having never seen the end of the video, Edward didn't know what to do except go to the second floor. He accomplished this much successfully and sat waiting on a sofa, where he watched a magazine.

'Hallo, Edward.' It was the girl from the interview corridor. She dazzled a smile his way.

'Hallo, Sophie.'

'What are you doing?'

'I was watching *Choice*.' He turned the magazine off. She sat down next to him.

'Why aren't you working?'

'Well, my video was blown up this morning.'

'Of course. Right. I see.'

'You don't know what I'm supposed to be doing, do you?'

'I'll have a look.' She fiddled with a wall keyboard. 'Here we are. Edward Wilson, room 102, tenth floor. You're meant to be up there.' She pointed heavenwards.

'Thanks.' He got up from the sofa.

'Fancy a drink after work?'

'Er, yes, OK. Where shall I meet you?'

'Don't worry, I'll come and get you,' she threatened. She

watched him amble off and smiled. 'A change is as good as a rest,' she said to nobody in particular.

A hand clamped on to her bottom.

'What was that you just said?' A tall good-looking young man was the owner of the offending hand. She peeled it off with some difficulty.

'Charles Dartmouth, what are you doing lurking in my corridor?'

'Who was that you were leering at?'

'Edward Wilson.'

'Oh, the new boy. Sir Desmond was talking about him yesterday. You don't waste time, do you? Fancy lunch?'

'No.'

'Dinner?'

'No.'

'Going bouncy bouncy together?'

'Admit defeat, Charles, and give us all a break.'

'I bought you these.'

'They're lovely. What are they?'

'Two tickets to *Comma, the Full Stop*. It's brilliant.'

'Charles, I've got work to do, unless you can tell me about Cumbria . . .'

'It's that new boy, isn't it?'

'Oh Charles, is that all you think about? Get me a leak on Cumbria, then maybe, just maybe, I'll come to the cinema. Goodbye.' She glided off. Charles didn't understand the meaning of the word 'no'. Such a lack of comprehension was spectacular in view of the thousands of times he had heard it from a woman's lips. He looked at the tickets in his hands and thought, *Change the bait*.

In Edward's office things were quiet. The monitor had told him to play some stupid game called Darthman, 'a multi-faceted complexal space odyssey battle game', which he had done for five minutes, after which he had gone for lunch. In the restaurant plaza he clapped weakly as some buskers finished an appalling mime act. He pushed his low-fat burger to one side.

'Hi. It's not Edward Wilson, is it?' A sandy-haired man of twenty-five was looking at him quizzically.

'Maybe.'

'Hi. Charles Dartmouth. Welcome to the Environment and all that blather. How's it going?'

'How do you know who I am?'

'Oh, I'm personal assistant to personal personnel department office.'

'I see. I'm fine, thanks. Settling in, you know.' Edward toyed with his coffee spoon. At a nearby table he spotted Sophie screaming with abandon as a young man was de-bagged. Charles sneered at them.

'I know her,' remarked Edward.

'Yeah, Sophie the life and soul.'

'Isn't she just.' Another shriek slit the air.

'No, you know . . . life and soul – mole. She's a department mole.'

'But if she's a mole and everyone knows, why don't they catch her?'

'It's her job. She's an official mole. Anything we want leaked, she leaks it.'

Edward looked at the group who surrounded her. 'They seem pretty obnoxious.'

'They have to be. They mix with journalists. Fancy her, do you?'

'Not really.'

'Sure about that?'

Edward had stopped listening. 'Not really. Sorry. Look, if you'll excuse me I've got to get back to my office. Goodbye.'

'What on earth for?'

'I've got work to do.'

'Good grief, have you? What work is that?' Charles fell in beside Edward and adopted a lazy gigolo pose.

'Darthman.' Behind, Sophie was lobbing ice cream at fellow eaters. She certainly enjoyed life to the full.

'Oh, Darthman. Right. Look, you don't want to go on playing silly video games. Hang on, don't walk so fast. Let's think up a job for you. Everyone does it. I know, you look a real sub-officer type.'

'I like Darthman.'

'Liar. I know, sub-officer for district . . . Come on, Edward, it's your job you know . . .'

'I think up a job?'

'Yes. Sub-officer for district . . . er . . . cooperation?'

'How about coordination?'

'Perfect. Brilliant, Edward. Sub-officer for district coordination. That's a plum post. Well done.' The lift doors opened. 'See you later.' Charles patted him on the back.

Back in Edward's office the monitor was showing a fat man holding a cheque twice his size whilst two teenage girls in bikinis rubbed up close to him with bottles of champagne. A washed-up personality mouthed soundlessly into a microphone. Edward turned it up.

'. . . and of course it's a dream come true for hubby and megadad of four, Jack Wallis. For sadly busty wife Brenda, supercook and wondermum, has to fly out with Baby Darren for million dollar medical treatment. But Jack will be bouncing with joy with this cheque . . . Have fun with this fabulous bonanza . . . and remember you played it on . . .'

Edward switched it off. Out of the corner of his eye he spotted an envelope slide under the door. He picked it up and opened the door. The corridor was empty. The envelope had a bright orange label on it: *For the attention of the Sub-officer for District Coordination*. Great, just great. He fished the contents out, a disk, and stuck it into his monitor. A military voice barked.

'Memo to the Sub-officer for District Coordination re the earthquake disaster of 1990 in Cumbria. You are required as sub-officer to make your annual inspection in the next forty-eight hours. Good luck.'

On 3 September 1990 Cumbria had suffered a substantial earthquake, 8.4 on the Richter scale. Later reports suggested a meteor or hurricane. Since that date bad weather conditions in the area had always prevented film being broadcast, so no one knew for sure what had actually happened.

There was a knock and his door opened.

'Hi.' It was Charles. 'How are you getting on?'

'I've been sent a memo as sub-officer for district coordination about Cumbria. They want me to go there. Ha-bloody-ha, Charles.'

'Struth, I didn't send you it. That's absolutely incredible, Edward.'

'Oh come on, Charles.'

'No, honestly. I've heard about this sort of thing happening before . . . When are you going?'

'I'm not.'

'You'd better. A request's a request even in today's Environment. Look, don't worry, I'll sign you off the Mainframe, but you'd better get going.'

Edward rose from the table. Oh well, he thought, nothing ventured nothing gained. It beat sitting around playing games. Besides, it might be fun.

Difficulties might come and go, but the inefficiency and disorganization of the national train service remained the rock about which the waves of social revolution broke harmlessly. Edward's feeling of excitement was therefore tinged with the usual dread reserved for those occasions when he travelled by train. He went to the entrance plaza at Euston and joined the end of the 150-yard queue to the one ticket booth that was operating. On the wall opposite, an enormous poster showed a train arriving through a shaft of sunlight in some charming country village. The tanned and handsome face of the stationmaster beamed down on the hands of his pocket watch. The slogan read: *We've got there.* Somewhere overhead a speaker crackled.

'Environment Rail apologizes for the late arrival of the previous apology. That apology was delayed due to staff illness. The next apology is running approximately ten minutes late. We apologize to passengers for any inconvenience this may cause.'

Ahead of Edward a small baby chirrupped the word 'twain' to its mother. The queue inched forward. He reached into his coat pocket and took out his watchman, screwing the ear plugs firmly into place. There was an old spy film from the seventies on Channel 38. He turned it up to shut out the 'twain' spotter.

'Don't you see? Zer can be no good wizout evil . . . no light wizout dark.'

'You're insane, Dr Zebra.'

'Ha ha ha ha ha ha ha . . . Brilliant perhaps, insane no.'

'Don't be a fool, you'll kill yourself and thousands of innocent people with the separation machine.'

'Stay back, I say . . . No . . . don't touch the lithium transducer . . . it's on a hair trigger . . .'

Edward felt a tap on his shoulder. The queue had evaporated; another train was cancelled. Only a middle-aged man in a flat cap stood between him and the ticket machine. The man seemed to be having difficulties in getting what he wanted.

'But I said a single to Carlisle.'

'Oh, well, that'll be £65,' it parried. 'Are you catching the 18:30 or the 19:35?'

'Er, the 18:30.'

'Well, you want the off-peak saver, that's £55.50. When are you coming back?'

'Friday morning.' He turned to Edward. 'Sorry, mate,' he said. Edward smiled good-naturedly at him.

'Well, if you're coming back on Friday you can do it on an off-peak super-save return, £42.'

'Hang on, I've got an elder person's "Get out 'n' about" card.'

'That's £21.'

'And I'm a member of Club 17 to 29.'

'£10.50.'

'I've got two travel-save vouchers.'

'£7.50 Cash? Or are you paying the easy way?'

'I'll pay the easy way, please. Sorry, mate.' Edward nodded. The easy way meant cross-checking, number verification and security inquiries. Eventually the machine bleeped and produced a small square of plastic. The man shuffled off. Edward squared himself to the microphone.

'Single to Cumbria.'

'£150.'

'I'm under twenty-eight.'

'Lucky you.'

'It's a Thursday.'

'So it is.'

'I'm catching the 18:30.'

'Not if you keep chatting like this.'

'All right, here.' Edward snapped his card into the machine and waited.

'We are a private company,' the machine remarked snottily. 'We're not here for your benefit.' A piece of plastic appeared. He took it and his card.

'Which platform is it?'

'The one with the train waiting on it.' The machine laughed maliciously.

'Next,' it blared. An old thin man pushed past Edward and squeezed his face up to the voice grill.

'Right,' he said gathering his breath asthmatically. 'I'll have an off-peak intercity over 55s but under 65s springtime sales shrinker megasave bargain buster night cruiser return ticket to Edinburgh on the 11:05, please . . .' He gasped for air.

'That's fifty pence.'

Sophie emerged from the comfort room with a fresh coat of lip gloss and a renewed determination to get some leak on Cumbria from Sir Desmond Riley. As she approached his office, Charles appeared hurrying in the same direction. He beat her to the door button.

'Just a minute, Charles Dartmouth. I was here first.'

'Sorry, Sophie. This is urgent.'

'Hah, I'm *leaking*.'

Charles looked her over. 'Let's put you in a bath and see where the bubbles are coming from.'

'Out of my way.'

'Just a minute, darling. You know that new boy, the one you fancy? Wilson, is it?'

'Yes.' She put her hands on her hips.

'I've got rid of him.'

'You rotten bastard.'

'To Cumbria.' Charles savoured the volte face.

'Charles, you are a genius.' Her voice was honeyed with pleasure. He grinned. 'Dinner tonight?'

'All right.' Visions of endless leaks from Wilson were already forming.

'You deserve it.' He reached but she was too quick. 'Pick me up at eight and don't be late.' She walked away.

Charles rubbed his jaw and pressed the entry button on the door. Table for two at Galtieri's, *mmmmmm*. The door slid back and he stepped through.

'Ah, come in, my boy. The Mainframe won't tell me anything. Is Cumbria all set to . . .' The door snapped shut.

2
FREEDOM IS CHOICE

The train left early to make up for all the late ones, and waited for an hour just outside Euston. Compared to the newly built centre the outskirts still looked rather shabby and redolent of the Difficulties. The stewardess left Edward in a window seat to have a nice trip and think quietly about the sudden turn his life had taken in the last twenty-four hours. He pondered deeply on the rusting tracks outside and fell asleep.

It was dark and the train had been moving for some time when he was woken abruptly by a thick Yorkshire accent which sat down loudly in front of him.

'You from the South?'

'What?' Edward tried to focus on the knobbly apparition, but focusing made no improvement.

'You were asleep, you were.'

'Yes, I *was*.'

'Well?'

'Well, what?'

'You from the South?'

'Yes.'

'Aye. Thought as mooch. So am Ah. Croydon, born an' bred.' This must be an example of the Northern sense of humour, thought Edward. ''Appen I've seen you on television?'

'No.'

'*Av've* bin on television. *God Loves You Show*. Didn't love me, though. Only won fifty pounds. Mind you, mustn't grumble. Ah've sin good times an Ah've sinbad, an' all in all Ah preferred the bad. Ahhhh, bot you wouldn't understand. *You're* from the South.'

'Yes.'

'So am Ah. Mind you, Ah've always felt close to the North. Ah've always felt Northern. Yer know, sort of ...' He turned his carbuncular head to the window and searched for a word in the darkness that roared past. '... Sort of ... miserable.' The misery filled him and his watery eyes poured it out over Edward in silent agony.

'Yes, I suppose there's not a lot to smile about in the North these days, is there?' snapped Edward, trying to put an end to the conversation and get back to sleep.

'There's not a lot of North to smile *at*, now that 'alf Cumbria's gone.'

Perhaps this man knew something. 'Really? What do you know about Cumbria?'

'Everythin'.'

'Really?'

'Aye. Went there once. It were all 'ills an' valleys an' lakes an' grass an' open sky with rollin' clouds, really ...' Again he searched the gloom. '... Really boring. Still. The Environment's a lot thinner at the top now. And at least that makes Scotland seem further away.'

'This is my first visit to Cumbria. I'm quite looking forward to it.'

'Yer won't like it. It's cold, it's damp, it rains, it's windy, it's primitive ...'

Edward gave way to sleep and didn't resurface until the train was grinding to a halt some hours later.

'... It's dirty, it's run-down, it's miserable, it's lifeless. Mind you, it's got its good points. The people are friendly. What we stopped for? Wipe the winder an' 'ave a look. What's out there?'

There was nothing but the same darkness that had inspired the words 'miserable' and 'boring'.

'Nothing,' observed Edward.

'Yer've arrived, then.'

A synthetic tannoy voice confirmed it.

'Will all passengers on official business in the Earthquake Zone please alight here. Will all other passengers please remain seated. Have a nice trip.'

Edward said goodbye, nice to have met you, and jumped on to the platform. The doors hissed shut and the train pulled away, leaving Edward in the miserable and boring darkness.

'Now. Which way, I wonder?'

'Ah don't rightly know. Bloody dark, in't it?' A strangely (over) familiar Yorkshire accent . . .

'What are you doing here?' demanded Edward.

'Just got off to stretch me legs an' the train pulled away. Still, at least we're together.'

'Yes, but I really must go.' Edward searched for somewhere to go.

'Down that bloody dark track wi' nowt at the end of it, Ah'll be bound.' Yorkie consulted his watch. 'Ah might as well come with you. Lead on, MacDuff!'

They stumbled along a gravel path that led from the platform.

'Ah don't rightly remember as we've bin introduced properly. Ah'm Gavin. Quite a popular name is Gavin in Croydon. Ever bin ter Croydon? Yer'd love it. *Ah* love it. The people aren't friendly, but there's a lot o' good things to be said fer it. Do you ever suffer from portentous nightmares? Ah'll give you a f'rinstance. You remember in the 'istry books that dream Martin Luther King 'ad? Well I had exactly the same dream last night. Ah wonder if that means *Ah'll* get shot?'

At that moment one of the new pilotless T7X fighter-jets of the Environmental Air Defence screamed over their heads at an altitude of about seven feet, and disappeared from view as quickly as it had appeared, which was fast enough. Gavin blinked at the sky.

'Bah 'eck,' said Gavin. 'That were one of them new pilotless T7X fighter-jets of the Environmental Air Defence.'

He marched on and tripped.

''Ere, 'ang on. Ah've just trodden in somat.'

'That was me.'

'Eulgh. Trust me ter tread in it. One little fighter-jet in t' middle of t' night an' 'e craps hisself.'

'No. You trod on *me*.'

'Gerrup. Yer a bit joompy, aren't yer?'

'Yes. Look, I'm hungry. I'm tired. It's dark. It's cold—'

'It's the North. Yer don't 'ave to tell me.'

It began to rain. Gavin smiled grimly.

'And it's beginning to rain. Lucky Ah brought my Pacamac.' He produced it proudly from his duffel bag. 'You're goin' to get wet.'

'Look,' said Edward. 'Why don't you just piss off?'

Gavin sensed that his new friend needed cheering up. He laid a fat, wet, plastic-coated arm around Edward's neck and began broadcasting his repertoire of Barry Manilow's greatest hits to the black hills around them. They set off through the night, pausing only to give airspace to the occasional passing fighter-jet.

On a long-playing record of Barry Manilow's greatest hits, precious moments of relief can be found in the silences between the tracks. Not so in Gavin's tuneless renditions. One song flowed mercilessly into the next. He was just entering his fifth and gustiest performance so far of 'I Can't Live Without You' and Edward was joining in with the umpteenth strained chorus of 'If You Don't Shut Up I'll Wring Your Bloody Neck', when Edward suddenly changed key and screamed an involuntary arpeggio similar to something that was currently in the Environment Top Ten. This was accompanied by a light-show in dazzling blue. It was over as soon as it had begun. Edward lay smoking in a puddle – though not to display a casual attitude to things: he was merely on fire. Gavin was awestruck.

'That was bloody brilliant. Ah *knew* Ah'd seen yer on t'telly. Do that again.'

Apparently Edward didn't feel like doing it again.

'All right. Suit yourself. Temperamental pop stars.' He stumbled onwards straight into the same electric fence that Edward had encountered moments before.

They lay smoking, each in his own puddle, for some minutes. Edward opened his eyes and winced. Brilliant white lights shone from every angle. They hummed powerfully, illuminating a long perimeter fence which stretched either side of a tall metal gate. The whole arrangement was fetchingly trimmed with barbed wire. Edward considered the possibility that he had died and was now at the gates of—

'Hallo!' A reedy, whining voice echoed camply across the hills from a forest of speakers. 'Can I help you?'

'Er. Yes please. I'm the district – hang on – I am the sub-officer for district coordination.'

'Bloody 'ell,' murmured Gavin semiconsciously from the other puddle. 'You never told me that. If Ah'd known Ah'd 'ave lent you me Pacamac.'

'Oh, we've been expecting you. You should have got the bus. I've got you on camera one. Just push the gate. It's open.'

Edward pushed the gate. There was another light-show in dazzling blue, and Edward performed a free interpretation of what used to be called breakdancing.

'Hang on a sec. It's still switched on. Now, where are we? Heat sensors . . . Microwave cameras . . . Infrared . . . Oooh. Here we are. Electric fence. Step through, Mr Wilson.'

Gavin was feeling unusually vulnerable as he regained consciousness. He looked at the sub-officer for district coordination from his puddle. Concussed, suddenly outclassed, and sensing a hint of hostility for the first time since they had met, he sniffed wetly.

'Are yer goin' ter leave me ter limp off alone across the black 'ills inter the cold night?' he asked innocently.

'Yes,' confirmed Edward. Gavin drew himself up from

his puddle, strolled off singing 'Copacabana' and was never seen again.

Inside the perimeter fence was a village of cubic concrete buildings set at odd angles. Each was numbered with bold black figures, covering a whole wall. The tannoy whined on.

'On your right – sorry, *your* right, *my* left – that's it. Can you see building number five? Follow the path round . . .'

A massive steel and concrete sliding door rumbled into life before him, and Edward entered a narrow, high-ceilinged corridor of bare concrete, pipes, cables, air-vents, automatic television cameras and fluorescent lights. The door boomed shut behind him.

'Now, down the corridor. Keep going. I've got you on camera four now. Can you see it? Ha ha ha!' Camera four winked obscenely. 'Hallo. Ha ha ha! Straight on. Five's on the blink. Can't see you now. Straight on . . . Straight on . . . Got you on six now. Straight on . . .'

Just as Edward thought he was being led to a dead end, the corridor turned sharply right. Here it was lined with numbered doors.

'Got you on seven, now. Fourth door on your left.' The fourth door on the left clicked open and Edward entered. It was a small cell, which boasted a bed, a sink, and nothing else.

'Everything you need's in here,' commented the tannoy helpfully. It really was all that he needed. 'See you in the morning.'

He crawled under the duvet and slept deeply, watched over by his invisible guardian on camera 41.

Shortly after dawn, a Mark 4 Fetcher, which until then had managed to bring into Edward's room a television, dry clothes and a towel without falling over or *dibidibidibidibing* too loudly, carried in a breakfast tray and simultaneously

31

tried to open a window over Edward's bed. Edward, who preferred hot tea through the mouth in his own good time, was woken by a whole potful searing through the duvet and into his flesh. Crockery flew as a fresh wind blew in through the window. For an awful moment Edward thought he must still be at home, and sprang into defensive posture.

'Eualgh!'

'I'll geb youd some more breakfast *dibidibidibidibi* . . .'

'Don't bother.'

'Oh goog,' mumbled the Fetcher from under the steaming duvet. 'Mifder Gendrigg's egsbegding you im moom firdy-four ad eighd o'clog.'

'Right, thank you.'

The tannoy guided Edward to room thirty-four on a getting-warmer-or-colder basis. He knocked tentatively.

'White hot!' squealed the tannoy.

'Enter!' boomed the resonant, projected voice of Kendrick, a man who had trodden the boards in the days when there had been boards to tread. Nowadays the practice of nearly all actors was to have an answer-phone and enjoy a sensible outdoor hobby. Seated behind his desk, the elegant and windswept trouper raised his eyes to the back row of some imaginary upper circle above Edward's head and with a long flourish and an odd rising inflexion boomed: 'Kendrick!! I exPECT you'll be WANTing your TOUR of inSPECtion . . .?'

Edward checked over his shoulder, but found no one else in the room. 'Yes. Yes, please.'

Kendrick drew a deep breath and darted a savage glance at seat S24 of the stalls, currently occupied by Edward's diffident face. 'You are no doubt aWARE of the discrepancy between the oFFICial and the UNofficial story on CUMbria?'

Edward nodded knowingly. How much was he *supposed* to know?

'Yes. Quite. I suppose it couldn't have disappeared in a nuclear power plant explosion, could it? Ha ha ha.'

Kendrick furrowed his brow. Perhaps it *could* have disappeared in a nuclear explosion. 'What do you mean?' barked Kendrick in one of his sudden shifts of gear for which he was nearly famous in his heyday at the Palace, Westcliff-on-Sea.

'Erm. I mean . . .' Edward was rescued by a grandiloquent backhand sweep of Kendrick's arm as he rose regally and pressed a button on the wall. A red velvet curtain drew itself up and sideways as on a great proscenium and revealed a large display screen showing a map of Cumbria.

'Cumbria has been sealed off, and for a very good reason. It is the home of a vast, top-secret social experiment.'

The map on the screen flickered and changed. A whole new town appeared in the middle of the Earthquake Zone. The picture closed in to display it on a larger scale.

'Ten thousand carefully selected men, women and children are living in an environment utterly defined by advertising.' Kendrick held one of his pregnant pauses, which once in his prime had been mistaken for a drinks interval. Edward stood uncomfortably, trying not to feel like the victim of a vast, top-secret practical joke. Had he heard right?

'Yes.' Kendrick slipped suddenly back into top gear. 'Advertising. We're trying to influence – and by that I mean *control* – the way people live, through information technology. Our commercial backers are simply quivering with excitement about our little project. Here in Cumbria, in the new town of Sellingfield, you only hear what we want you to hear. And I hear the experiment is nearing a perfect conclusion. It's for the good of us all.' Kendrick, his arms outstretched and with the veins protruding from his temples, surveyed seats A1–A45 of the gods. 'We're WORKing towards the IdEAL society.'

Edward grasped the nettle. 'You mean life here is like a permanent cornflake advertisement?'

'Exactly. All day. Everyday. For everybody.' White flecks of spittle were forming at the corners of Kendrick's mouth. 'Full of sunshine. Whiter than white. Secure in a sound investment. The *natural* way. That's the Sellingfield PLEDGE!' Kendrick launched a bold thumbs-up signal somehow inconsistent with his otherwise classical style and held it trembling in the air, before bowing his head, exhausted, to the thundering, non-existent applause.

'Thanks,' offered Edward uneasily. 'I can't wait. How do I get there?'

'Just follow the Yellow Brick Road.'

'Aha,' said Edward, to show that he appreciated the joke even if he hadn't understood it.

'Yes. Originally the main entrance was a huge wardrobe, but there were problems with the lorries, so our PR people came up with the Yellow Brick Road. Inspired, isn't it? Out of this door . . .' He swept open a door at the side of his office and like a conjuror's assistant presented a Yellow Brick Road which lay just to the left of a huge, derelict wardrobe. 'Sign here.'

He produced a stiff plastic document from his breast pocket. A light pencil was attached to it by a length of wire. Edward fumbled for his ID card. 'What's it for?'

'Oh, the usual. If anything happens, it's all your fault. That sort of thing.'

Edward ran the pencil over his card. The plastic signalled acceptance, offered Edward a copy of itself and wished him a wonderful day. Kendrick bade him farewell and Edward made his way over to the Yellow Brick Road.

The telephone on Charles Dartmouth's desk trilled with an urgency it rarely had cause to display in his sleepy office. Charles snatched the receiver with one hand and held his throbbing head with the other.

'*Yes?* Sorry, Environment here. Charles Dartmouth speaking.'

On the screen an elderly man was hurriedly adjusting his toupee.

'Ah. Hallo. Sellingfield, Kendrick here. Just seen a chap. Claims to be the sub-officer. Edward Wilson. Doesn't have a clue. Is he kosher?'

From his own office, eight floors above, Sir Desmond was watching in on the call with keen interest.

'You're sure, Kendrick? Edward Wilson, you say? Have you let him in?'

'Yes. He's on his way now.'

'I'll send someone up to check him out.'

'You'd better give me his name.'

'She's called Sophie.'

'Thank you. Goodbye.'

Sir Desmond was too slow to get off the line and found himself facing Charles. 'So, Charles. Wilson out of bounds already? Excellent. Have you notified SSN?'

'No. Didn't have time. Bit of a night last night.'

'Well, just for once, forget your extraordinary love-life and get on to them. I'll send Sophie in to see you. And I suppose I'd better try to deal with the Mainframe. God, I hate computers. So much to be done. Do you understand these things, Charles?'

'Treat 'em like a woman. Just tap the keys and hope for the best.'

Sir Desmond had never understood women either, and Charles had never felt the need to try. They agreed to talk it over in the communications room later, when they had dispatched their respective tasks.

Charles tapped out a long number. A scrambled image from Picasso's Blue Period appeared on the screen. Charles switched on the descrambler and from the disorder burst the serious, red face of a young man with an exploding hairstyle and round tortoiseshell glasses.

'SSN HQ.'

'He's arrived. He's called Wilson. Start the operation now.'

'We need more arms!' The young man raised his arms as if to prove it.

'You'll just have to do the best you can. Find Wilson and take him.'

'How?'

'I don't know. Use the quick-behind-this-bush method, and don't damage him. Goodbye.'

It was always best to be curt with these SSN people, besides, Sophie had slunk into the office without knocking as was her infuriating habit, and seemed silently to be accusing Charles of something, though for the life of him he couldn't think what it was. It must have been something to do with that dinner he had well and truly earned and enjoyed with her last night.

'Look, Sophie, whatever it was, I'm sorry. I had a bit too much last night, I think.'

'More like not enough, lately.'

'Look, Sophie.' Charles switched to charming mode. 'That Wilson. He's arrived in Cumbria, and I've managed, don't ask me how, to get you assigned to him.' Sophie's pretty green eyes beamed greedily.

'You catch up with him. And if anything unusual happens, leak it back to London straight away. You can get a flight in half an hour.' She was already strutting down the corridor to the lift. Edward Wilson was hers, for a few days at least, and Cumbria, the moles' holy grail, was within her grasp.

Blissfully unaware of the fate that was being arranged for him, Edward stood on the Yellow Brick Road Moving Walkway, which whisked him along at twenty miles per hour past some of the most exhilarating scenery he had ever seen, and all to a selection of tunes from *The Wizard of Oz*. First there had been a tiny Venetian port built on an artificial lake with underwater lighting in pink. The surrounding houses gleamed immaculately in a field of astroturf. Then there was an Alpine village with steeply gabled roofs and a ski-lift to the top of a giant helter-skelter sculpted into the hills. Concrete goats grazed contentedly. Ahead, mirror-glass towers of outrageous design glinted in the morning sun. The moving walkway led to the very centre of the miracle town, directly to the entrance of the biggest building by far. Over its vast steel portals, in gigantic neon lettering, were the words

MEGAMARKET ENTRANCE ONE: CHOICE IS FREEDOM

Inside, where the soft musak was massaging the air, hundreds of ideal men, women and children drifted to and fro as if in a dream. Each bore an identical smile that revealed perfect teeth. Each was blessed with clean, shiny hair with added bounce. It was simply perfect.

'Hallo.' Edward turned to face a winning smile with a gentle Welsh accent and petite figure swathed in a tight blue uniform. 'Are you lost?' As winning smiles go, this one was winning hands down.

'No. Not yet. Well, I might be.'

'I'm Megan. It's my job to look after all the visitors. You'll like it here, and if you don't, we'll want to know why. That's the Sellingfield Pledge.' She gave the thumbs-up signal like a right hook. 'Take one of these.' She produced a sheet of paper. Edward took it. It was a lovely shade of pink. Megan clearly approved.

'Seventy-three per cent prefer that colour to any other. Mmmmmmmmmmm.'

'Mmm.'

'Mmmmmmmmmmm! It makes filling in an ordinary questionnaire seem really fuddy-duddy.'

Edward looked closely at the sheet. He had taken it to be a sample of wallpaper.

'This is Megamarket entrance one. What's your first impression?'

'Well, it's . . .'

Megan laughed a pretty, trilling laugh. 'Oh, don't tell *me*. Tick one of the boxes for question one.'

Besides each question was a column of multiple-choice answer boxes. The answers to question one were:

A   SUPER.
B   FANTASTIC.
C   WONDERFUL.
D   AMAZING.
E   MMMMMMMMMMM!

'Mmm,' pondered Edward.

'Mmmmmmmmmmmmmm!' enthused Megan. 'Most people choose that one. Come on. There's so much to see and do in Sellingfield. This is the Megamarket. One square mile of choice. And this way . . .'

She led Edward across a broad piazza towards an expanse of green that might have been a recently restored section of the Garden of Eden. Megan gushed the merits of Sellingfield life in wild ecstasies of statistical hyperbole. Edward was having some difficulty keeping up with the pace of both speech and movement. He found himself gasping as they arrived at the gates of Paradise.

'And here is the leisure park. This is where the fun-run trail starts. It's for all the family, from Gran to tiny tots.'

A trim elderly female with a blue cotton and polyester tracksuit and matching rinse shot past them like a gazelle, followed by Mr and Mrs Kellogg and their two children.

'Let's run part of the way, past the boating lake and towards the sports centre,' suggested Megan. And before Edward could take in the full horror of the idea, she had shot off at a brisk Olympic ten thousand metres pace, extolling the wonders of Sellingfield as she went. Edward panted in her wake.

After a half a mile of this, Edward, feeling queasy and out of breath, slowed to a halt where the trail wound through a thicket. Megan's shrill tones faded into the distance.

'Psst.'

Edward glanced around him. Nothing but bushes.

'Pssssst! Over here!'

Edward peered into the foliage. 'I'm sorry?'

'Over here! Behind this bush!'

'Where?'

'*Over here!*'

Edward stepped towards the source of the urgent whispers.

Strong hands forced him down into the thicket to meet the serious red face of a young man with an exploding hairstyle and round tortoiseshell glasses. Edward's first instinct was to seek escape.

'Get down! Thank God you've come. Take this.' The young man pressed a warm metal object into Edward's hand. For an assailant to provide his victim with a lethal weapon whilst molesting him in a thicket needed some kind of explanation, but there was no time for that.

'I'm Jenkins. Follow me.'

Edward wondered why he was still taking the orders, since he appeared to have the upper hand.

'Where to?'

'It's a big cheeseburger in the sky.'

At this point Edward decided to stop trying to work out what was going on. Maybe it would all make sense later.

Jenkins, his mysteriously trusting abductor, led him crouching through a densely wooded part of the park, glancing furtively at the sky. The reason soon became clear. A helicopter thundered overhead. Edward was getting to be an old hand at this sort of thing, and flattened himself into the undergrowth, but Jenkins pulled him up sharply. He stood erect, smiling a broad Sellingfield smile, and waved at the helicopter, whispering urgently through clenched teeth, 'Helicopter! Wave!'

'Wave?' repeated Edward, lamely.

'Shut up. Just wave and smile.'

Edward waved and smiled. The helicopter passed low and hovered. The pilot, a muscular middle-aged man with a prominent jaw, returned the greeting and flew on.

'Phew. That was close. Follow me, friend. And mind where you're pointing that thing. It's loaded,' warned Jenkins, leading him deeper into the wood.

Megan turned to present the glittering sports centre with restaurant and bars to her charge but was disappointed.

'Where the hell has he got to?' she asked herself.

At precisely the same moment, Sophie was asking herself the same question. Since her arrival at Sellingfield she had asked sixteen ideal citizens and seven uniformed guides if they had seen a worried-looking twenty-seven-year-old male with bad posture and slight hair loss anywhere in the town. They all took it as a joke and claimed their prize. She was about to devote her investigations to Sellingfield itself, when she spotted a uniformed guide outside the sports centre, although this one looked a bit lost herself.

'I'm looking for a visitor. His name's Edward Wilson.'

'Oh, I've just lost him. I think. Are you a visitor?'

'Yes. Where do you think . . .'

'You'll like it here.'

'But I must find . . .'

'And if you don't, we'll want to know why. That's the Sellingfield Pledge.' Megan presented a proud thumb and handed Sophie a questionnaire. Sophie grasped the paper. After all, it was a charming shade of pink. Megan began her guided tour where she left off, and Sophie followed, gazing at the sheet.

Edward and his abductor arrived at the far edge of the wood. Before them stood a giddyingly tall glass tower, topped by what appeared to be a gigantic wholemeal sesame

40

bun, filled with one hundred per cent ground beef and a slice of cheese.

'It's a big cheeseburger in the sky,' observed Edward.

'Yes. Cheeseburger Tower. Our hide-out. The rest of the group are waiting for us in the cheese layer.'

'The *what*?'

'The group. Our group. Us. We'll have to take the lift. The stairs are broken.'

They entered through a side door and pressed for the lift.

'Just the two of you, is it?' it moaned in synthetic 'London cabby'. 'Which floor, guvnors?'

'Cheese layer.'

'Righto, guvnors. Cheese layer it is, then,' it conceded reluctantly and ground upwards. 'What is it you lot do in this place? It's not ready for occupation yet.'

Edward too was wondering what sort of meeting could be taking place inside a layer of processed cheese. 'I'm afraid I don't know. You'll have to ask him.' He waved his gun absently at Jenkins.

'Any old way, you're not supposed to be here. No one is. It's more than my job's worth even to open the door for you.'

Edward turned to Jenkins. 'Well, what are we doing here? And why am I carrying this gun?'

The lift screeched to a halt. 'Gun? Did somebody say "gun"?' Lifts have ears but no eyes. They also have a nosy disposition and conservative sense of propriety. Jenkins held his hand over Edward's mouth.

'No. Nobody said "gun".'

'Cor. That's a relief,' sighed the lift as it resumed the ascent. It is almost impossible to fool an alarm clock or a security door, and there are toilets that won't take shit from anybody; but a lift will believe anything. 'I thought for a moment you must be part of that revolutionary group that meets in the cheese layer.' The lift opened on to a vista of sickly yellow. 'Cheese layer.'

It was a vast, square room with yellow-tinted glass walls that matched the carpet and the ceiling, and had a panoramic view of Sellingfield. On about four dozen yellow plastic stacking chairs in a far corner sat the revolutionary group. They were engaged in angry debate. Jenkins led Edward into their midst. Each revolutionary bore the sad, dreamy, earnest look one might expect to see at a gathering of the Flat Earth Society awaiting a guest lecturer from NASA. They shouted furiously at each other, gesticulating extravagantly and paying no regard to the new arrivals.

Jenkins raised his hands.

'Friends.'

The debate continued.

'*Friends!*'

The debate raged on.

'FRIENDS! MR WILSON HAS ARRIVED!'

In the sudden silence, Edward stood gaping at forty-seven faces that gaped back in wonderment. A tall man with a bow-tie and a squint rose to greet his messiah. 'Tell us our plan, O Great Leader!'

'Please grow up, Clarke,' pleaded Jenkins, as if for the umpteenth time. He turned gravely to Edward. 'It is time. Better tell them the plan, Mr Wilson.'

Edward felt it was time for a multilateral laying down of cards on tables. 'What plan? I've been dragged here against my will and now you want a plan. There's been a terrible mistake.'

Clarke rose again, released the safety-catch on an automatic rifle and squinted through the sight at Edward. 'A traitor! Judas! Are you with us or against us?'

'I wouldn't upset Clarke if I were you, Mr Wilson. He's mad. Just tell them the plan.'

Edward blanched. There is an old television commentators' adage: Open your mouth and hope for the best. Edward, who hadn't heard it, was about to invent it anew. 'Er . . . The Plan . . . Er *the Plan* . . . Er . . . Mr Chairman,

Ladies and Gentlemen. I call this meeting to order . . .
Ermm . . .' Edward felt that he was losing at match point.
Beads of sweat erupted all over his body. 'Erm . . . Can we
have the minutes of the last meeting?'

A high backspin lob to the baseline has a similar effect:
reprieve or salvation. The minutes box was produced and
switched on. Its synthetic female voice pervaded the saffron
air with aching concern.

'Minutes of the Smash Sellingfield Now group, Wednes-
day the 13th of December 1993. Brother Clarke apologized
for his absence and was duly appointed Munitions Officer.
The group re-affirmed its commitment to the violent overthrow of the Sellingfield Project. There was a short break
for light refreshments. Brother Ossipon remarked that if
everybody paid their subs on time we might be able to buy
the nice biscuits with the light creamy centres, but until
then we would just have to make do with plain digestives
and stop complaining. This was seconded. Brother Ossipon
said he would name no names, but those of the group who
were spoiling it for the others would know who they were,
obviously, and cough up. The group reaffirmed its commitment to the violent overthrow of the Sellingfield Project
again, and agreed to await final instructions from a secret
leader who would come amongst the group when the time
was ripe. The group reaffirmed its commitment to the
resistance of all advertising slogans. Brother Clarke said
this would take a lot of bottle. The group agreed nem. con.
and adjourned to the Sellingfield Milk Bar.'

Faces turned eagerly to Edward. He began to feel faint.
He cleared his dry throat.

'Brothers and sisters. Friends. The Revolution (ahem)
will start erm, tomorrow.'

The group cheered.

'Er, victory is ours.'

They cheered again. The mind is said to be at its most
lucid when faced with death. Edward's reminded him that
he hadn't eaten since yesterday lunchtime, which wasn't a

lot of help. He took a deep breath. It might have been his last.

'Meanwhile, let's get some food in and have a party!'

They cheered deliriously. A pre-revolution fork supper – only a true leader could suggest such a thing. The sheer audacity and brilliance of it! Some stood on their chairs to shout suggestions for the party snacks and drinks. Others very sensibly suggested paper plates and binliners. Edward was nominated and then seconded to go and get everything. There was an eagerly fought election for the post of Guide to the Revolutionary Leader, and after two recounts Edward and his new guide were carried shoulder high to the lift and sent on their way with a shopping list.

In the lift, his new guide introduced herself as Susan and embraced him with an adoring passion. The idea began to grow in Edward's mind that it might not be a bad idea to stay on as Revolutionary Leader. Until after the party, anyway.

Outside the Megamarket, Susan passed him the shopping list with furtive *legerdemain*.

'I'll meet you outside entrance twelve. And keep a low profile. Try to blend in. Keep smiling, and if there's any trouble – run. Have you got the gun?'

Edward was shocked to discover he was still carrying it.

'Yes, about this gun—'

'Wave. And smile!'

A helicopter flew low across the sea of ideal shoppers. Edward waved with his free hand and smiled dutifully. 'Why are we doing this?' he asked out of the side of his mouth. The helicopter passed on.

'We all live in brand-new, super-modern, fully fitted houses. So when the nice man in the helicopter flies over, we all wave and smile,' explained Susan.

Puzzled, Edward strode into the Megamarket and blinked in the fluorescent glare, which was brighter than the midday sun outside.

A glossy red electric dumper truck with a wire-mesh

loader sensed Edward's arrival and introduced itself politely.

'Hallo. I'm Eric. I'm your shopping buggy for today's buying experience. Just hop aboard and I'll take you round the Square Mile of Choice.'

Edward climbed into the seat and they began their journey into Consumers' Wonderland.

'Where would you like to begin?' asked Eric deferentially.

'Well, I'm having a party.'

'Perhaps we should start with French bread, then. The Gay Paree Plaza. It shouldn't take long. It's about half a mile.'

Eric's monitor flashed up a map of the Megamarket. An arrow pointed to a blinking red dot.

'You are here,' said Eric comfortingly. 'Follow the dot on your monitor and you won't get lost.'

Eric and Edward whirred past hordes of beaming shoppers mounted on buggies. They were busy discussing the relative merits of kitchen systems with the Megamarket guides, who noted their opinions and led them through a labyrinth of kitchen fittings.

'There's so much freedom to choose,' gushed a woman, as Eric passed on into The Land of Nod bedding area, where a couple's opinion on the subject of beds was eagerly sought by yet another guide.

'In that case, what in-bed facilities do you regard as essential to a good night's sleep? Tick boxes A, B, C, D or E.'

'Gosh, darling. What do you think?'

'Oh . . . I really don't know. They're all very nice.'

'I know,' whined the guide. 'But we value your opinion. Most people choose "E".'

'Mmmmmm. Yes. All right. "E".'

On they whirred, past an array of Home Exhaust Systems, all declaring their advantages over each other and offering prices with synthesized homely voices.

'I practically fit myself!' called one in desperation, as

Edward and Eric moved through to Fetcher World. A spokesman Fetcher raced from the display stand and blocked their path.

'Hallo.' The voice was even more sickly-sweet than that of the Mark 4. 'I'm the new Mark 5 Fetcher, and I don't fall over . . .' It fell over. '. . . quite as often as other Fetchers do. I'll fetch *any*thing for you,' it promised, lying helplessly on its back. A massed chorus of Mark 5 Fetchers on the surrounding display stand sang the new Fetcher jingle, to the tune of 'A Four-Legged Friend':

> A Fetcher is Faithful,
> A Fetcher is true,
> The new Mark 5 Fetcher
> Has fallen for you.

They all fell over and lay giggling in a heap.

'Drive on, Eric.'

Eric ploughed a path through to Menswear, then Soft Toys, Children's Daywear, Children's Evening Wear, Outdoor Gardening, Indoor Gardening, Outdoor Sports, Travel, and finally the Food Hall, which was divided thematically into Old Bombay, Tokyo Town, Peking Palace, Little Italy, American Pie, Safari Park, Gay Paree Plaza, Old Sellingfield and the German Garden, where a team of Fetchers in lederhosen was entertaining a group of happy shoppers with a slap-dance performed to *Die Götterdämmerung*.

Eric halted at French Bread in the Gay Paree Plaza. Even here the choice was endless. An animated rubber mannequin with a banded sweatshirt and a black beret waved from the top of the Pierre Boulanger Baguette Stand.

''Ello. Ah am Pierre Boulanger. Ouelcome to mah fabuleuse range of French breads – bread for a perty or just for eeting.'

It was interrupted by another rubber mannequin in a farmer's smock on the Dorset Farm Stand. 'Ar . . . Yew

46

don' want that thar furrin muck. Yew wants French bread from a Bruttish bakery. Troi moi Farm 'ouse Baguette.'

'Is there any difference, Eric?'

Eric displayed a table of statistical results on his monitor and arranged them into a fourteen-colour histogram.

'As you can see, this morning's opinion poll suggests that seventy-three per cent of the bread-buying public prefer Pierre Boulanger to any other leading brand.'

'Rubbish!' bellowed the Dorset farmer. Edward took an armful of baguettes from Pierre's stand and dropped them into Eric's basket.

'Now,' said Eric, 'how about some pâté? And we'll need some wine, crisps, cheesy nibbles . . .'

'Binliners,' added Edward helpfully.

'. . . Binliners, paper cups, paper plates . . .'

Eric's basket was brim-full as they headed for the check-out. There another bewildering range of choice awaited: Fifty Items or Less; Fifty to Two Hundred Items; More than Two Hundred Items; Credit Only; Cashcard Only; Easy Instalments; Staff Discount; Credit Coupons; and Don't Knows. Eric recommended the Don't Knows, because that had the shortest queue and offered Edward a range of entertainment facilities on his monitor to help him to enjoy his queueing experience. There were films, games, news, bargain of the week . . . Edward chose to catch up on the news.

The presenter was so cheerful about the news, she was all but singing it.

'. . . on the stock market today, the latest take-over has sent Environment shares literally through the roof after a slow start this morning. Another bonanza for the people. Meanwhile back home in Sellingfield, a new opinion poll suggests that opinion polls are the most popular way of giving your opinion. Your chance to give your opinion on this is on *It's Your Opinion*, which has been moved to the more popular time of two o'clock. And lastly the story of *that wedding*, watched live by millions of soap fans last

47

night between real-life actor Simeon Grange and fictitious character Bev Kinch. After the extraordinary show-business wedding, the first of its kind, real-life actress Tanya Rogers, who plays barmaid Bev, explained at a press conference that, though she wouldn't dream of marrying Simeon Grange herself, she had great respect for Bev's feelings as a character and wishes her happiness in her new series . . .'

Edward was now about halfway down the queue. Some young marrieds were sitting behind him in a two-seater buggy, with TERRY and SAMANTHA written across the front. Terry was gazing at their haul.

'Well I *think* that's just about everything, darling.'

Samantha glanced up from her horoscope on the monitor. 'Mmm, the trolley's full!'

'Ah, well. Must be, then.'

Samantha turned her adoring eyes to Terry. 'Aren't we lucky to have so much choice?' she cooed.

'Yes. And freedom. That's the Sellingfield Pledge.'

They gave each other a simultaneous thumbs-up and fell on each other laughing at the extraordinary coincidence.

'Do you know what?' said Terry. 'Tomorrow morning at the crack of dawn, I'm going to get my wellies from the boot of that lovely luxury saloon that appeared in our double garage the other morning, along with the folding bicycle, and I'm going fishing in some of that beautiful countryside that's so close to our fabulous new home.'

'Yes. Sometimes I think you only came here for the fishing! When you get back, there'll be lots of cheap hot water and Nuts 'N' Bran Cracker Breakfast.'

'Mmm! Helps give you fitness and vitality.'

'I'm taking the children windsurfing this afternoon and then we can choose a new colour scheme for the lounge.'

'Mmm, yes. That'll take *hours*. There's a completely new range of country colours.'

'And we'll have to choose the best part of the Megamarket to buy them from . . .'

'. . . with a whole new range of consumer magazine disks to help us.'

'Next please.'

While Edward had been absorbed, Eric had been inching towards the check-out.

'My customer is about to enjoy five hundred and nineteen pounds, forty-five pence worth of quality goods,' announced the shopping buggy proudly.

Edward fed his cashcard into the till. It bleeped and whirred. And fell silent. A red light flashed on top of the till. Heads turned. Edward darted an embarrassed glance at Terry and Samantha, who stared back in mute amazement. The musak stopped in mid-phrase. Edward felt his sweaty grip tighten on the gun in his pocket, as an ugly murmur spread like a wave through the line of shoppers. Edward had been rumbled. How or why he had no idea. An earsplitting fanfare rent the air, and an announcer's voice burst into the echoing Megamarket.

'Cashcard holder Edward Wilson?'

Whatever it was, Edward didn't feel like staying to find out. 'Eric! Get me out of here! Fast!'

The buggy obeyed instantly, but it wasn't designed for speed. Edward jumped off and ran for the exit, his ears buzzing with fear. The announcement continued.

'Edward Wilson! Five hundred and nineteen pounds, forty-five pence is this month's lucky price! And that makes you this month's winner of the Sellingfield Megamarket Cashcard Bonanza!'

But Edward heard none of this. A carnival atmosphere swept over the throng of shoppers. They gasped. They cheered. Some had already begun to show signs of panic, while others pointed towards the fleeing figure of Edward.

The announcer continued to whip the excitement into a frenzy.

'Now, Edward, all you need is for the first person who has spent more than five hundred pounds today to shake you by the hand and say "Congratulations, Sellingfield is the best for choice!" and you and that lucky, lucky person will share in the fabulous bonanza!'

Thousands of ideal shoppers formed an impromptu stampede, as others dashed at random between the display stands to fill their shopping buggies to the required minimum value of goods. Eric, like all shopping buggies, had been longing for the day when he would be stolen from slavery and left to rust happily at the bottom of the nearest canal. He followed Edward with a devotion only the sub-human can manage, a devotion that could only lead to martyrdom. Oblivious to the passions that boiled within the breast of his closest pursuer, Edward turned in a moment of indecision in the doorway. A roar crescendoed behind him from a tide of bobbing red faces, each with an identical manic smile and screaming 'Sellingfield is the best for choice.' They were gaining. Edward shot across the piazza towards the leisure park, resolving to take up a more regular programme of fitness in future, and weaved like an asthmatic rabbit along the Fun Run Trail towards the clump of bushes and the thick wood beyond, with five hundred and nineteen pounds and forty-five pence worth of award-winning goods hard on his heels. Turning the sharp corner in the bushes, Edward collided painfully with a blue-uniformed guide and her client, who was filling in a pink questionnaire. Smoke poured from Eric's rear as he braked to avoid a multiple pile-up.

'Edward! Where have you been? You look terrible.'

'Sophie! What are you doing here?'

'Looking for you.'

The ground was thrumming under their feet. The advancing army was dangerously close.

'Look, Sophie, no time,' gasped Edward, waving the gun. 'Eric, you keep to the path, and go like hell!!' The loyal machine obeyed his liberator, trailing clouds of blue smoke. 'Sophie and er, you . . .'

'Megan.'

'Megan. You'd better come with me.'

Both women gaped at Edward, transfixed by the gun. As obedient hostages should, they followed him into the bushes, just as the screaming horde tore past in hot pursuit of Eric's plume of smoke.

Edward, Sophie and Megan thrashed through the undergrowth in blind terror until they came unexpectedly to the edge of the boating lake, where several canoes lay conveniently beached. They paddled inexpertly, but with great determination, towards safety at the other side of the lake. Too exhausted to speak, they clawed their way up a steep embankment in search of sanctuary. Edward was first to the top. Directly below was the burning shell of Eric, surrounded by a mass meeting of demented shoppers, each shaking the other by the hand forcibly and howling 'Sellingfield is the best for choice' like a plaintive mating call.

Edward watched in awe. But for half a second longer than he should have. One of the shoppers recognized him, and led a charge. Seeing a steel door in the side of the slope, which, miracle of miracles, was open, the hapless trio charged down a flight of steps into a dark tunnel. They scrambled and panted endlessly through the blackness.

'Ohgodohgodohgodohgodohgod!' wailed Sophie.

The end of the tunnel came abruptly and was discovered by Edward, who ran into it, then by Sophie, who ran into Edward, and then by Megan, who ran into them both. Above them was a long metal ladder. They climbed frantically, spurred on by the reverberating footsteps and shouts of the mob in full pursuit. The ladder seemed of unreasonable length. In the darkness and in his state of near-exhaustion, Edward estimated that they had climbed at least a hundred feet above ground level.

'Why are they chasing us, Edward?'

'Do you want to stop and ask, Sophie? Aaaaaaaagh!' Edward's head found the cast-iron lid. With his last remaining strength he heaved it open, to find himself on the roof of the Megamarket. They scrambled into the sunlight. Megan took over the lead towards the emergency staircase. But the trap door had already begun to spew out screaming consumers tottering like hysterical ants from a nest.

Edward sat down. 'Enough is enough,' he whimpered.

Neither Megan nor Sophie was in any state to question his resolve, or lack of it, and reeled onwards as the pack closed in. Sophie glanced back remorsefully to catch Edward's last moments. And had an idea.

'Use the gun, Edward!'

Delirious, Edward took the disembodied voice to be divine guidance. He pointed the gun in the air.

'Keep back!' he croaked at his pursuers, who were staring heavenwards and waving.

'I warn you!' he warned, firing a warning shot. It was a direct hit. In silence the good citizens of Sellingfield watched the helicopter fly on in a shuddering ball of flames, then plummet on to the Sellingfield power station, which exploded mightily. A giant mushroom of smoke blackened the sky.

Susan, the revolutionary Edward had left waiting outside entrance twelve of the Megamarket, and who had not quite kept up with the pack, emerged from the tunnel and took in the situation instantly.

'People of Sellingfield,' she declaimed. 'Long live Mr Wilson! The revolution has begun.' The consumers cheered wildly at this new variation of the game.

Inspired, Susan pointed to their new future. 'Mr Wilson shall lead us to freedom!'

'Mis-ter Wilson, Mis-ter Wilson!' chanted the crowd. But Edward had gone.

With newly discovered resources of energy, Edward had fled down the emergency stairs and out of the town centre. As he reached an area of wasteland near the perimeter fence, he could hear the intermittent gunfire and the odd mortar shell in the distance. Fighter-jets screamed through the air, strafing buildings and occasionally each other. He could also just make out the barking of dogs. They were trailing him.

'Mr Wilson! Over here! Jump!' It was Clarke. Edward jumped over a low ridge and landed in Sellingfield's main refuse channel. Clarke was standing up to his bow-tie in it and holding a pump-action rifle.

'Brilliant!' he declared. 'Me and the great revolutionary leader in the thick of it together.'

The barking was getting nearer.

'What you need is olfactory camouflage,' advised Clarke.

'What's that?'

Clarke took a handful of thick, dark sludge and smeared it hurriedly over Edward's face and neck. 'That'll hold 'em off. You run and I'll deal with them. You must survive to build the new world we have fought for.' Edward waded out and ran, as Clarke removed the pin from a grenade and hurled it.

In the cheese layer of Cheeseburger Tower, those of the revolutionaries still waiting for Edward to return with the food and drink were growing restless. After all, they had homes to go to and families who were expecting them – and then there was the telly. After a prolonged game of I Spy and the passing of several constitutional amendments to the SSN Charter, they fell to debating the group's revolutionary slogan. The argument that a group whose fundamental aim included the abolition of slogans should do without them was dismissed as counterproductive and unrealistic.

'Let us first build a society where such things as slogans are a thing of the past. Only then can we go forward and put our own house in order, but until then we must fight fire with fire,' proclaimed Jenkins.

'Bit long-winded for a slogan,' said Ossipon airily. 'How about "Victory Is Ours!"?'

'That's no good. Supposing we lose? How can we keep face?' groaned a bearded dwarf at the back. 'We'll have to use something less presumptive, more open-ended . . .'

'All right, shorty,' interrupted Ossipon. 'How about "Victory Might Be Ours, If We're Lucky"?'

'Typically asinine, typically male,' screeched a pair of baggy dungarees from under a woolly hat. 'What's all this nonsense about victory, anyway? Victory and defeat, dominance and suppression, sadism and masochism, product and consumer! Typical dichotomous dualism: them and us, male and female, you and me, Goldilocks and the three bears! God, can't you see? It's all the same thing. It's what's oppressing all of us. It makes me feel sick. Sick, sick, sick. All of it. And here we sit arguing amongst ourselves! What hope is there? None! Unless we all get together and do something about it!'

Three other woolly hats cheered.

'*Do* something? Like what, for instance?'

'We should all join hands round the Megamarket and sing a nice song. And I'll talk to the press. They're bound to turn up.'

'How can we join hands round a building one mile square?'

'We could space ourselves out.'

'We'd be standing a hundred and fifty yards apart. No one would even notice us.'

'How about "Join the Revolution and Bring a Friend"?'

'Rubbish!'

'How about "We Can Make It Together"?'

'Sexist!'

'Sexist! Sexist! Sexist!'

'Listen to that! And *she* wants to talk to the press! I've got a degree in media studies, and *she* wants to talk to the press. *Her*. Why should the press write about her when all she does is repeat herself? Can you imagine *her* talking to the press?'

'Oh shut up!'

'How about "Revolution – For the Man Who Doesn't Have to Try too Hard!"?'

'Ha, bloody, ha, pig!'

'And *me* with a degree in media studies.'

'Hang on. Shut up, everybody!'

'*You* shut up!'

'Sexist!'

'No. Just shut up! Please! *Shut up! Did anyone hear that noise?*'

'No.'

'Well, I did. An explosion.'

They ran to the window. The fire that followed the explosion in the power station was spreading rapidly, and there was a riot on the Megamarket roof. Jenkins was furious.

'They've started the revolution without us.'

'Typical,' said one of the woolly hats.

'It's not fair,' said Media Studies.

Jenkins, who had always believed that humankind should seek change through gradual revolution and not through violence, felt his blood boil.

'I'll show those bastards,' he cursed, smashing the window with the butt of a rifle and letting off several rounds. 'Hypocrites!' he screamed.

Back at the Department of the Environment, Sir Desmond Riley reached lazily for his phone and listened with detachment as Kendrick barked the news of insurrection in an ecstasy of panic.

'Thank you, Kendrick. I'm sure you're all doing your best. That will be all.' He replaced the receiver as Charles breezed in carrying a sheaf of papers.

'Ah, hallo, Charles. Your boy Wilson's done the trick all right. Ahead of schedule too. I was beginning to think that SSN lot would never be able to do it.'

Charles suppressed a look of shock. How could he have managed it? He wasn't even briefed. *Damn.* That wasn't the idea at all.

'Charles, are you all right? Got the papers ready?'

'Er, no. I mean yes. But er whoops, damn. I've brought the wrong headlines. I'll have to go and get the new ones, I mean, the right ones.'

Charles returned, looking flushed. He spread the new papers across Sir Desmond's desk. They were the front pages of the next morning's papers, as yet empty of copy, but each emblazoned with a headline. The *Sun*, the *Guardian* and *The Times* bore respectively the following:

SPY SEX REVOLUTION GUN BATTLE!
ENVIRONMENT CONCERN OVER EXPERIMENT

and

SPY SEX REVOLUTION GUN BATTLE!

Sir Desmond was pleased. 'Better get Sophie to leak the story asap, Charles.'

Deep within a safe recording bunker in Sellingfield, an engineer switched to emergency power and gave the thumbs-up through the glass panel. Sophie cleared her throat to deliver the leak of a lifetime.

'Official leak four three seven stroke B for immediate release. There is positive evidence of an illegal social experiment in one of the Restricted Zones. The Environment had been totally unaware of the antisocial nature of this project until it was brought to light by a revolt among its thousands of victims, led by a plucky have-a-go hero. The Environment has pledged a full internal inquiry. Right. That'll do. Laser it back to London. Now. Can I borrow one of your helicopters?'

Edward was cowering in a ditch crying and chattering to himself about the pleasure of home food and warm beds, and not making himself feel any better, when a bass, juddering *whomp, whomp, whomp* enveloped him. He felt a fierce wind. He looked up, grinned pathetically and waved.

'Don't be an idiot!' blared Sophie through a megaphone. 'Climb up the ladder and get in. Sophie's taking you home!'

3
CHOICE IS PROGRESS

Though Edward's home was not the haven it should have been, at least it was quiet. The silence was broken only occasionally by the sound of machines burping and belching as they digested their daily electronic fare. The Fetcher had remained under the canopy of clothing that had trapped it the day before. But there was a limit to its patience.

'Alarm, when do you think Edward is coming back?' it inquired.

'That depends where he's gone.'

The Fetcher considered this. But not for long. It was very, very bored. With an effort it released itself from its bonds and whirred into the lounge. It surveyed the carnage of the SASagram and decided to tidy up. It was six o'clock and the television flicked itself on. A young man was smiling with a gold map of the Environment revolving slowly behind him. The words 'News Jive' glittered at the top of the screen.

'Wow. Six o'clock on Channel 16. I'm Garry Wayne and I've got a hangover. Get this, news jivers. Main stories today: revolution in one of the Restricted Zones, the do-it-yourself baby kit, and the Fetcher who tried to get a mortgage. Details after this.' The screen dissolved into a commercial. In forty seconds there unfolded a story of marital discord, financial recriminations, abused children and adulterous relationships. Then a tall, trustworthy-looking gentlemen of the old school turned to the camera and said: 'If you can't trust your spouse, trust us, Marples, Drew and Cavendish, the "Lawyers Who Care".' Most people would have trusted him with their lives. The newscaster returned looking even more excited.

'Pow. There's been a revolution in one of the Restricted Zones against a sinister doomsday experiment using real human guinea-pigs. Secretly called the Sellingfield Project and conducted without the consent of the Environment, it's now the subject of a full inquiry. Although called "Project Death" by some, little is known about what exactly went on in the area which once suffered a devastating earthquake. However, a spokesman for the Environment made the following statement to the press a short time ago.'

The TV flicked to an official-looking old man standing in an official-looking office flanked by official-looking people. In his right hand he was holding a copy of a popular newspaper.

'STRING 'EM UP BY THEIR BALLS'

read the headline. In grave tones above the noise of the spinning motor drives he assured the press that such sentiments, though understandable, mustn't hide the real issues that had arisen. The result of the in-depth inquiry would be available for the nine o'clock news, he pledged.

'Well, that's nice to know,' said Garry. 'And, of course, contributions for the victims of this disaster are already pouring in to a special fund, so please, please, please, please, please, get on the phone now and pledge some credit. NOW. OK. We'll be giving you the number to ring a little later on in the show. Now let's go live to Brent Cross Shopping Mall, where Marie Media is talking to you about the disaster.'

'The Sellingfield Project – sinister. That's what I think. It's not right is it?'

'I think it's terrible. Thank goodness the Environment's looking into it . . .'

'Well, it's nutty, it's covered in chocolate, fills me up nicely.'

58

'What? You mean "Project Death"? String 'em up by their balls, that's what I say . . .'

The screen returned to Garry, now vying with a backdrop which screamed:

'HOW DID IT HAPPEN?'

in vast cerise capitals.

'Now one effect of the disaster has been the decision to introduce more opinion polls to protect the Environment from any repetition of this sort of thing. So if you want to give your opinion now, phone in and, hey, while you're at it, pledge something for those who are suffering now.

'How? That's the question on everyone's lips when it comes to the new do-it-yourself baby kit. A special report next. And, of course, Freddie the Fetcher who's falling over to get some bricks 'n' mortar. All that in a couple of minutes.'

The tragic matrimonial problems of the Bran family returned.

The telephone buzzed and Edward's face appeared on the screen.

'Fetcher!' he bellowed above the roar of the helicopter. 'Fetcher, I know you're there. Come out and speak to me. Now. Or else.' The Fetcher remained behind the sofa, safely hidden.

'Come out from behind the sofa! Listen, you piece of junk. I want a hot bath when I get back in about half an hour. So do it, OK? And clear all that rubbish up. I'm bringing someone home.'

'Oh,' chimed the alarm, 'may we be permitted to know who?'

'No, you may not. Well, Fetcher? We haven't got all evening.' Edward put the phone down in the cabin and dropped his head back into the capable hands of Sophie, who pillowed it gently. She resumed dabbing gently at the small graze on his forehead with disinfectant, and kept a lazy eye on the autopilot.

'Owwww ... take it easy, Sophie.' She shushed her wounded hero.

Meanwhile the Fetcher had set about the assigned task with the zeal of a medieval grail-hunter. It sprinted around the flat on its wheels, flicking machinery on, checking the bath, consulting the fridge, and getting the champagne into the ice bucket. The latter task was finally accomplished without breakage on the eighth bottle. It was just returning with a bucket of hot, sudsy water to wash the television, when it noticed the bath had failed to shut off. It crept to the edge of the bathroom door and watched the water-level rising.

'Er, bath, can you turn off, please?'

'You bet. Hope he likes it hot.' The water rose still further, lapping at the rim. 'Well, what do you know. Edward must have hit my panel a bit too hard. Ha ha ha ha ha. The switch is broken. I can't stop the water.'

The Fetcher let out a high-pitched alarm and reversed back into the lounge. The water had broken over the edge of the bath and was now beginning to flow copiously into the room. The Fetcher's domed head revolved. Meanwhile the television was beginning to ship hot soapy water from the bath and from the bucket the Fetcher had up-turned in its haste. It emitted a spectacular sheet of orange flame and followed it up with black, oily smoke.

'Oh no, the TV's on fire,' squeaked the Fetcher.

'Aaaagh! I'm on fire!' agreed the TV.

In the kitchen the fridge had opened its doors to the oncoming tide, fruit and vegetables now bobbed and ducked on the swell. Only the alarm remained above the chaos and was putting through a call to the emergency services.

'No, that's Bluff Cove ... No B ... B ... as in break-water ... What do you mean you can't hear? There happens to be a flood here ... Flood ... F for Freddie ... Freddie? ... No that was just to explain the letter ... The letter F ... There *is* no Freddie ... Look ...'

At that moment the smoke detectors, which had been a

model of self-restraint, could contain themselves no longer and tripped the sprinkler system. It filled the air like a tropical monsoon. It streamed down the walls. It pelted into the rising tide. It put the fire out. Edward would be pleased.

'Drink?' The question wafted through the clouds of steam to Edward, who lay in the bath with a hot face flannel stretched over his face.

'Mmmm.' She dimmed the lights, lit a candle, fetched up glasses from beneath the bar and started to concoct two multicoloured drinks with little umbrellas and cherries. Two of these, and most moles were below ground. She took one over to a table and sipped carefully from the other. She couldn't help smiling, recalling Edward's face when they had returned to find his house gutted and sodden. It had shown the pathos of Chaplin, the madness of Hitler and the colour of Lazarus. After the injection they had discussed his situation and she had insisted he come back with her. In fact, the ambulance crew only undid the straps on that condition, considering the ferocity of his attack on the Fetcher. In the train the drugs had calmed him down and relaxed him completely. She found his reaction to it all rather sweet, and felt protective. In the bath Edward was wondering how to get off with her.

'Drink is ready,' she shouted as she swayed into the hall to check the answer-phone.

Edward lifted the face flannel and squinted through the steam. He had dropped off briefly and was for a moment disorientated. The last ghastly twenty-four hours leapt back into focus. He shuddered. His earlier tranquil life seemed an eon away. He eased himself out of the bath, grunting and puffing like an old man, and wrapped a towel round his battered frame. Rubbing the mirror clean of steam he opened his mouth and said 'Ah.' He looked terrible. He cast around for a razor. There was only a can of Silhouette, 'the Smooth One'.

'How do I look?' he asked the mirror.

'Great.'

Ego boosted, he slipped into a robe and pressed the door button. He spied Sophie in the hall. She smiled and waved him into the lounge. It was, as he expected, very feminine: lots of pastel shades and wicker things. His Molotov sat smouldering on the table. He picked it up and took a gulp. It was like being hit on the back of the head with a rubber club. The next moment, however, the burning in his belly died down and the world began to look more cheerful. He turned on the telly, which was showing a popular sitcom. As the throbbing subsided, he wiped his eyes and settled his thoughts on the hospitable Sophie. It would be convenient if she fancied him. But Edward always lacked confidence when it came to women and relegated all hope to the forlorn category. One thing did bother him: her surprise appearance in Sellingfield. He found it hard to believe it was a coincidence. He took another sip at the glass with all the wariness of a gazelle at a waterhole. It didn't seem so bad second time around. He resolved to ask her about Sellingfield as soon as she had finished listening to half the male population of London on her answer-phone. The sitcom drivelled on and Edward gazed at it, lost in thought.

On the answer-phone screen in the hall, a drunk Hooray was slobbering over a pint.

'God, you're never in. Amazing. We're all drinking down at the Belgrano. Why not come? Bye!'

Charles Dartmouth was next to appear.

'Hallo, Sophie. Look. There's a party tomorrow to see in Difficult Day. Dress eighties and bring a can of wine. I'll pick you up and ... Sir Desmond was pleased with Cumbria. Don't you think I deserve a little reward?' Sophie grimaced. That Charles had all the subtlety of a sledge-hammer. The Hooray returned, drunker and more vociferous.

'Hallo, Sophie. God, you're still not in. Henry's as ratted

as a dog.' Behind the caller, Henry could be seen ratted as a dog.

'Oh no. He's debagging me, the swine!' The green corduroys dropped to reveal boxer shorts spotted with Perrier bottles. 'Oh no. Henry's been sick.' Sophie turned the machine off. Enough was enough. She took a swig and turned to join Edward.

'That was Charles Dartmouth on the phone. There's a party tomorrow for the Difficulties. Shall we go?' She eased herself down next to him on the sofa. Edward wondered what all this 'we' business was. He also wondered why with four sofas in the room she had to squeeze herself next to him on the smallest.

'I don't mind,' he said, in answer to her question.

'That's what I like about you. You're so decisive. What's this on the telly?'

'Oh. It's *Keep Your Chukka Up*, the polo sitcom.'

'That's my favourite. It's so funny. Turn it up.'

Two aristocrats in riding gear were striding round a studio set.

'Not –?!' exclaimed one.

'Yes! Some plucky sucker's played his last chukka!' Taped laughter dinned.

'Not . . . Chaz the Spazz from Buckingham Pazz?' More prerecorded chuckles.

'We'll have to be quick. Where's Suzie?' Enter Suzie.

'Has anybody seen my pussy?' The taped response went berserk and stopped dead.

'Ah, Suzie. Forget your cat. We've lost all our chukkas.'

'That must have made your eyes water!' Canned delirium and an explosion.

'Oh no. The marquee's exploded!' Hoots of artificial exultation.

'I'll kill your mother!' Thunderous applause and jolly signature tune. The credits rolled and another staggeringly popular episode finished. There seemed to be nothing but polo on the telly nowadays. Sophie reached for Edward's half-empty glass.

'Top-up?'

'Mmmmmmmmmmmm.'

'Next on Channel 24,' announced the Channel 24 announcer, '*Bonkers in Honkers*, the madcap escapist comedy about merchant banking in Hong Kong.'

'Oh. Turn it over.' The television sensed Edward's mood and switched to a sombre presenter, backed by sinister music and some old footage of grim social unrest.

'The day after tomorrow sees the annual celebration of the Difficulties. Difficult Day this year will be marked by a record number of parades, demonstrations, riots, strikes, power cuts and shortages. Channel 18 will be covering the event on the day, all day, the length and breadth of the Environment, and we'll be out with our cameras bright and early at four o'clock for the opening ceremony in Cheltenham.'

Sophie sauntered back with glasses brimming and squeezed herself back on to the sofa.

'Hardly room for two,' said Edward.

'I know.' She snuggled closer. 'What's this?'

'Oh. Something about Difficult Day. Do you want my cherry?'

'Yes, please.' She sucked on the proffered cocktail-stick.

'Sophie . . . What were you doing in Sellingfield?'

'Why? Did you think I was following you?'

'No. I just wondered, that's all.'

'Oh. Isn't the result of the inquiry on any minute? Take a look, television.' Sure enough, a spokesman could be seen standing outside the Environment Building under film lights.

'. . . and the report concludes that the Environment is in no way to blame for the series of tragic mistakes that resulted in the setting up of this experiment. Had the computers been operating correctly, the huge power drain could have been accurately plotted. It goes without saying, of course, that this kind of thing cannot and will not happen again. That's the Environment's Pledge.' He presented an upright thumb.

'Well. That's a relief, isn't it?' said Sophie, heaving a sigh. Edward shook his head, drained the last of his glass and grinned across the guttering candle. They were both drunk.

'Darling, let me show you where you're sleeping.' She waved a hand and sent a glass spinning. 'Let me help you to my feet, I mean your feet. Let you help me to your feet. No –' They staggered around in the gloom. 'Here is your room,' she said, after they had circumnavigated the flat twice. They weaved in and Edward disappeared from sight completely. He had found the jacuzzi. Sophie shrieked as he flayed the air and rose and sank in the foaming water. It was either an uncanny impersonation of a drowning man, or . . . She crouched by the side and heaved him out. He lay sprawled on the carpet, chest heaving. She raised a clenched fist and applied heart massage. It *had* been nothing more than an uncanny impersonation of a drowning man, but Edward had been laughing too hard to explain. Sophie extended the field of operations to amateur hot-water-bottle inflating. Edward tried to signal that his pulmonary system was working fine without assistance, but she laboured on like Florence Nightingale on Benzedrine. As she began to slacken the pace, Edward summoned his strength for concerted self-defence. His arm encircled her neck with a passion that surprised and delighted her. Her mouth closed over his once more. He gave up the struggle and settled to the task in hand. Things were looking up.

They fell to re-living mutually incompatible scenes of passion from recently remembered soaps. But the night's activities passed without undue embarrassment and eventually they gave way to a deep, drunken sleep.

Edward woke first. He lay on his back smiling into the night. The nape of Sophie's neck lay cradled on his right arm. He watched her breasts rise and fall. In a funny sort of way he felt paternal towards her at that moment. He suddenly realized that he didn't even know her surname.

'Edward.'

'Mmmmm?' He rolled off his back and laid his arm across her. Her fingertips traced the outline of his spine.

'Get me some fruit juice from the fridge.'

He nuzzled closer. 'What did you say?'

She giggled. 'Oh go on . . . I'll say thank you when you come back.'

He slipped the sheet off and picked his way across the carpet.

'Remain exactly where you are,' an iron voice commanded. Sophie screamed and Edward did as he was told, frozen in the middle of the room. His stomach felt as if it had hit clear-air turbulence.

'Halleluiah!' a choir of a thousand voices thundered.

The iron voice reverberated again.

'This is the Totally Reverend and Wholly Holy Dr Calvin saying stop and come to Jesus!' Edward got back into bed. The choir halleluiahed. The television burst into life. The screen was filled by a rugged tanned face with cold blue eyes and a stetson which had a large, silver crucifix glinting on the crown.

'We're broadcasting to you live from the sanctified studios of Jesus Gulch, Utah, to look into the lives of these two sinners . . . these animals . . .' He spat. 'These fornicators!' The dutiful flock whooped and hooted.

'Go away,' Sophie whispered.

'The Lord gave us life, bread and water. He also gave us microwave technology and satellite communications. And through these gifts, we and our audience of ten million believers around the globe have been watching you doing . . . it.'

They gulped.

'Go ahead. Gulp, sinners!'

'But it's, it's immoral,' Edward stammered.

'Shuddup,' sang the massed choir in perfect unison.

'Repent and come to Jesus. Stop drinking. Utter no foul words – especially that short one that begins with *F*. Stop fornicating *now*!'

'We weren't doing anything wrong,' protested Sophie. Edward wasn't too sure.

'Ten million Christian witnesses can testify that you were.'

'Oh for God's sake let's turn him off,' she implored.

'For God's sake let's leave me on!'

Edward scrambled for the remote control, found it and pressed the off button. There was no response. He pounced towards the TV and the massed choir gasped in unison at his nakedness.

'See!' howled Calvin. 'He has the mark of the Devil! Or, or something very like it.'

Edward tried the manual switch.

'See how their sin has found them out!' Calvin cackled. 'Watch them panic like rats in a trap.'

Edward yanked at the socket. It came out of the wall and the harangue stopped.

'. . . Squirming like pigeons from hell . . . They unplug their TV set so we speak to them through their radio.' Edward snatched it from the bedside table and dashed it to the floor.

> 'We are one,
> We are strong.'

The alarm had been called in to the crusade. Sophie threw it in the jacuzzi.

> 'We are love,
> We are truth,
> We are clean,
> We are pure,
> Unlike some,

We could mention,
And God is on our side.'

Blared the toaster: 'Any donation no matter how large will help us to stamp out sin. Our credit-card lines are open, and remember helping the Lord is tax-deductible. And now a word from our sponsors . . .'

'Did you know that Charrington Ballistics produce some of the best missile . . .' Edward threw the toaster through the window. They waited for another appliance to proselytize them. But there was silence, save for the January wind that whined through the broken window. The technological limits of the Church of the Latter Day Inquisition had been reached. On the bed, Sophie sat with her legs tucked up to her chin.

'Oh God, come back here.' Edward pulled the sheet from the floor and swirled it around the two of them. They clung together. Sophie managed a weak smile which broadened slowly.

'Let's teach him a lesson.'

In Jesus Gulch, the Totally Reverend and Wholly Holy Dr Calvin took the Lord's name in vain.

Sir Desmond sat fidgeting in reception on the top floor of the Environment Building. He watched the secretary working at her terminal. She looked up nervously.

'Oh, how remiss of me. More coffee, Sir Desmond?'

'No, thank you.' Why was her coffee always so bitter? he thought. He preferred the fuller flavour of mellow Monmartre, *mmmm*. He checked through the fat file he had brought with him. It seemed to grow everyday. God, he hated these Tuesday meetings. He felt like a schoolboy of nine up before the headmaster on some conker fraud. What was worse was having to dress as one. The secretary jumped at the sound of the intercom. Poor thing. Her nerves had gone working for *him*.

'*He*'ll see you now.'

'Thank you.' He rose and adjusted his satchel. The secretary scanned his attire scrupulously.

'Is that a paperclip on your file?'

'Yes, should I . . .?'

'Yes, remove it. It's been paperclips all week, I'm afraid, so don't . . .'

'No, no . . .'

'. . . even mention them.' The paperclip was consigned to the blazer pocket.

'Oh, and your shoes. Remove them.'

Sir Desmond moved towards the door.

'*He*'s got yellow tights on today,' she added. 'But on no account look at them.'

The door slid back and he padded down the soundless, brightly lit corridor, its walls bedecked with movie idols of the fifties. At the end a further door opened as he reached it. He stepped through into an enormous, richly carpeted room. It was simply furnished, with a huge marble desk at one end with two computer monitors on it. The walls were light grey and entirely unadorned. A huge plate-glass window stretched the length of the room – a good hundred yards or more, giving the finest view of London. At the centre of the window stood a man of about sixty-five. *He* wore a grey suit jacket and canary yellow tights. *He* was the man on all the posters. In real life *he* had shock-white hair – not fashionably grey like *his* public persona – which *he* kept parted down the middle. In *his* right eye there was a monocle.

'Ah, Sir Desmond, my trusty myrmidon.' The voice was soft but carried menace with it. 'I understand the weather is unusually clement for this time of year.'

'Erm . . . yes.' Outside it was freezing.

'Although I never leave this room. Come in. Come in. Ironic, don't you think, that wedded as I am to the Environment I should never experience it at first hand.' *He* raised his left eyebrow at Sir Desmond.

'But you have the farm.'

'Ah yes, the farm.' *His* good eye became dreamy. 'One day I hope to see the farm. They tell me it prospers. So little time. And Difficult Day upon us once again.'

'Tomorrow.' They stood facing one another forty yards apart.

'Come, come, don't waste my time. Presumably all the arrangements are made?' Sir Desmond nodded.

'It must be the biggest and most impressive so far. The Difficulties must be relived at least once a year. They need to be reminded, you know. They would forget their own names if they weren't told every day.' *He* padded across the vast room to a huge scale model of a shopping centre. It was the size of a large town.

Sir Desmond dropped his voice. 'Is this the new Megamarket?'

'Yes. Pretty, isn't it? The results of the Sellingfield Project are fantastic. Just think, one of these in every town. The real work is beginning. The London Megamarket will be ready in days.' *His* eyes were afire. *He* turned to Sir Desmond for his comment.

'Consummate consumerism. The ideal society.'

'Eloquently put, my naughty understrapper. From the ashes of Sellingfield, the phoenix of a new Environment will arise like a great mythical bird.'

He beat his arms lazily. 'Aaaark, aaaaaaaark.' *He* smoothed back a lock of hair that had fallen forward. 'I want no flies in the ointment. There are none, I trust?'

'No, we used a new chap for Sellingfield, called Wilson. The Mainframe's putting him on Flexispace. Riddle is dealing with it.'

'This Wilson. Is he bright?'

'I thought he was an idiot, but he scored over eight thousand points on that induction game.'

He digested this. 'Mmmmm, needs watching.'

'Yes, we've got a mole on him. Sophie. She's got on the job round the clock.'

The monocle popped out of *his* eye. 'I saw them on American television last night. The boy's an idiot. And an exhibitionist. Paperclippy.' Sir Desmond found himself staring at the tights and shot his glance.

'Will that be all?'

He looked at Sir Desmond pensively. 'They're trying to poison me, you know.'

'Who?' asked Sir Desmond.

'The poisoners,' *he* replied airily. 'Oh, the burdens of office. It is a lonely life.' *He* screwed the monocle back into place and fixed *his* eye sombrely on Sir Desmond.

'Sir Desmond, my erk.'

'Yes?'

'*Hold* me.'

Sir Desmond stepped towards him.

On the second floor of the building Edward was trying to wedge his card into his office door, which stoutly refused to accept it. Earlier in the day he had been taken shopping by Sophie to replace all her broken goods from the previous evening. She took longer than anybody he had ever gone shopping with to buy anything. After that there was the usual army of pollsters to battle with, and finally they had run into Charles, who insisted they tell him all about Sellingfield over a platter of croissants at the Port Stanley. Every now and then Edward had caught him sneaking sly glances at Sophie. Twice Edward had taken her hand, but let go after a polite inquiry from an elderly couple about last night's screening of his fledgling sex life. Edward decided to leave Sophie to shop alone.

He had one last go at the door. His patience snapped and so did his card.

'Morning. Wonder if I can be of assistance?' An over-weight, middle-aged man who smelt of breakfast was standing by his side.

'Well, my keycard has been rejected and now . . .'

'Oh, that's terrible, rejection, terrible.' He squinted at the card. 'The important thing is not to take it personally. Morning, Colin.' Colin walked past without a flicker. 'Suit yourself – the name's Riddle. What's yours?'

'Edward . . .'

'Still, you've got to laugh, haven't you? You married? Any kids?' He took out a battered Polaroid. 'Beautiful, aren't they? That's Barry, Kevin and Tamara. Morning, Ian.' Ian looked the other way. 'Git.'

Edward tried again. 'Do you think my office has been moved?'

'What I always say is: Who cares? The Environment is all around you.' He scratched his bottom. 'In any case, they changed it all this morning. What's your name? Mine's Riddle. Unusual name that. I've dined out on that name, you know.' He looked at Edward for a reaction.

'Really.'

'Yes. It's – it's on my credit card.' Riddle was racked with laughter. The overweight frame shook hideously. 'Still, all changed now. Flexispace. That's progress. Look. If the world was the size of a pea—'

'What is Flexispace?'

Riddle looked pained. 'I'm *explaining*,' he said with a sniff. '. . . and the sun was a football, and you put them in a bath, which represents the solar system, and assuming you had enough hot water. Right? Let's see . . . Bath, pea, football . . .' He collected all the elements on his fingers. There was a pause. 'I've forgotten it.'

'*What's* Flexispace?'

'I was wondering if you'd ask me that. It's sort of . . .' He rummaged in his jacket. 'Here's a leaflet.' He handed it to Edward.

FLEXISPACE
A NEW CONCEPT FOR LIVING:
LET US GIVE YOU THE FREEDOM

TOGETHER WITH THE GIFT OF FLEXITIME
TO WORK WHENEVER, WHEREVER, AND HOWEVER,
OR NOT.

ISSUED DEPT ENVIRONMENT™ 1994

Edward passed it back.

'What's your name, then,' asked Riddle.

'Edward Wilson.'

'Oh. You should have said. You're on the pilot scheme.'
He handed over another piece of paper.

PARTICIPATING MEMBERS OF THE PILOT SCHEME:
EDWARD WILSON

Edward felt at a loss. He had only just got used to the whole new concept of having an office and going to it for a few hours a day. Now there was Flexispace.

'I only just got my own office,' complained Edward.

'What do you mean? 'Course you've got offices. You got a choice of about one hundred thousand offices. What's this fixation about offices, anyway? You a bedwetter? Look, the whole building's yours. Right down to the thirty-eighth basement level. It's a staggering prospect.' He handed Edward a further piece of literature:

FLEXISPACE: A STAGGERING PROSPECT

'My wife left me last week. Didn't even leave me a note.' The man looked as if he might break down. 'Still. At least I've got my health.' He gave a raucous laugh, which brought on a coughing fit. 'What I'd do if I were you is wander round the building and do anything you fancy.'

'I haven't got much choice, have I?'

'Haven't got much choice?' Riddle was flabbergasted. 'You've got more choice than ever. It's all about choice – choosing, selecting, happy hunting ... And remember: They also serve who only stand and wait. Read that on the back of a crisp packet. Tara!' Riddle watched after Edward.

'Opinionated little creep,' he spat.

Edward stepped out into the corridor. He had taken
Riddle's advice and was commencing Flexispace from the
thirty-eighth basement level. It was badly lit and reminded
him of old spy films where the hero is trapped by heavies
and has to fight his way out. Down here the monitors only
worked spasmodically. Ahead, a door opened and a face
appeared.

'Excuse me,' it said. 'Saw you coming. Who shot
Liza?'

'Who's Liza?'

'What do you mean? Oh, I get it. Nice one. We'll use
the old amnesia-in-a-car-accident alibi. Thanks.' The door
slammed shut. Edward tried it. On the other side was
another corridor with ducts running off it. In the distance
Edward could hear voices, and decided to investigate. Soon
the corridor opened into a chamber the size of an aircraft
hangar. It was bisected by a wooden partition right up to
the high ceiling. In the middle of the partition there was a
door. Edward opened it and wished that he hadn't. He
stood blinded by lights of dazzling intensity. They gave off
a terrific heat. A woman's voice – American, bitchy and
hard – cut the ether.

'Oh. So you've come back to me, you pathetic little worm.
Don't you see, I can never respect a man who needs help
with his lobster claws?' There was no doubt that the tirade
was directed at him. He squinted through the light. A
stunning blonde in her late twenties stood just a few yards
away, glaring at him. Her prodigious chest rose and fell.
Her eyes rolled like tumble-driers.

'Look at me, you reptile. I'm a woman. Well?'

There was no doubt in Edward's mind.

'Yeah. Take a good look . . . And I have the needs of a
woman.' She ran her tongue over glistening lips and flared

her nostrils. 'You and your shoelaces! It was your idea to shoot Liza, wasn't it? You whom I *once* loved.'

Edward registered the name Liza. 'Now, wait a minute. I—'

'Oh. So you deny it?'

'No. All I said was—'

'Oh. So you deny it?' Her head was rocking metronomically.

'Look. It's got nothing to do with me.'

'Oh. So you deny it?' She pointed a crimson-tipped finger at him. An effete male voice wafted from behind the lights. 'Cut, cut, cut, cut, cut, cut, cut, cut! I thought I said clear the set, Jocelyn.' A woman wailed an apology. 'Who is this merry andrew?'

'I'm—'

'Are you a complete moron?'

Edward tried to make out who and what was behind the lights. 'No, I'm not, actually—'

'Oh. So you deny it?'

'Sebastian. Switch off that bloody actress, would you?' Striding towards Edward was a tall man in his thirties. He wore jodhpurs and a tee-shirt which announced: 'CAUTION, EGOMANIAC'. Around him milled a gaggle of acolytes. He examined Edward and let out an exasperated howl. Turning to his assembled court he pointed at Edward with one hand and planted the other on his hip. 'William, I can't work under these conditions. I'm an artist. I don't want to make soap operas. I want to make *adverts*. I have talent. Clear the set and get rid of this cretin.'

Edward watched fascinated as a group of technicians unscrewed a plate from the actress's midriff. One of them stuck a power cable into her buttock.

'I didn't realize you used robots.'

The assembly burst into titters.

'You didn't imagine we used *real* actors, did you?' snorted the director. 'Now, if you would be so kind, we've got the "Susan – isn't – getting – fulfilment – from – Gavin –

75

because – he – hasn't – come – to – terms – with – his – father's – homosexuality – but – doesn't – realize – it's – not – his – baby" scene next.'

The director and crew strode back to the cameras. Edward trooped along behind them, trying to look inconspicuous. The set was adjusted and the actors positioned. The director lifted a megaphone to his lips.

'Action.'

'Vee Tee rolling.'

'Oh, Gavin. Can't you see I love you? Why reject it?'

'Susan. Don't you understand? How can I come to terms with my life knowing that my father is gay? For all I know I could be the same underneath all this. What if I left you and our baby for another man?'

'Gavin. About the baby . . .'

'Yes, darling. That beautiful, innocent child who must never know.'

'It's not your child. I had the baby with Russell. He was present at the birth while you were drunk in that bar.'

'Russell? Russell? But he's the man I love. The man I was going to see tonight.'

'Cut!' shrieked the director. 'Right. I want the set cleared so we can shoot Liza. And get rid of *him*.'

Soaps guarded their plot-twists with the care of Swiss banks. Edward was thrown with great energy out of the studio.

Edward picked himself up in the corridor. Two men were marching briskly towards him. The one in the lead was a spry septuagenarian with tortoiseshell half-moon spectacles and a tee-shirt displaying the gates of heaven and the slogan: 'I'M UPWARDLY MOBILE'. The second man limped just behind him. His face looked as though it had been hewn from pig-iron by a blunt instrument. The tall septuagenarian had spotted him.

'Zo. Good mornink. Zere you are. Vell, come along. And don't shilly-shally. Follow me.' Edward fell in behind them.

They walked on in silence. The tall man glanced back at Edward and halted abruptly.

'Who the hell are you?' he asked.

'I'm—'

'Don't vorry. I'll remember. I'm Dr Erikson, and zis is Spung. He's my chum. Ve do everysink togezzer, you know. Vell . . .' He sought to qualify. 'No, no. Just about everything.'

Spung made the sound of a thirst-crazed water-buffalo and Edward took this to be a laugh.

'Say hallo to Spung.' Edward extended his hand. 'But don't touch him.' Edward retrieved it smartly. Spung leered at him and stood on tiptoe to whisper in Erikson's ear. The doctor smiled sagely and resumed walking.

'Now zen, Edvard. If I were to bring out a new washing-up liquid, vat should I call it? It's new, and it makes things really . . . er . . . Oh.' He searched for the word. Spung ummed and erred in sympathy.

'Clean?' said Edward. Erikson's eyes lit up.

'Brilliant. Make all your dishes clean, vis CLEAN. Edvard, you are a natural. Zere is a great future for you.'

They came to a door inscribed with the words 'Environment Creative Policies Department'.

'Ze Bright Ideas Department,' announced Erikson proudly. He opened the door and ushered Edward inside. A small group sat in animated conversation around a large oval desk. Spung strained upwards and cupped his lips to the doctor's ear. Erikson frowned.

'No. *I* found him. Spung wants to introduce you, but I think I'd better. No one likes Spung.' Spung nodded enthusiastically. Erikson clapped his hands. 'Now. Everybody stop and listen, please. Zis chep, whose name I can't remember, vants to choin us, don't you, Vatsyourname? Edvard. Zere. I told you I'd remember.'

There were murmurs of dissent which Erikson attempted to quell. 'And already he has come up vis a name for zer new cleaning agent. Go on, whoever you are. Tell zem.'

77

Edward looked at a sea of expectant faces. It was like the Sellingfield Revolutionary Group all over again. He took a deep breath.

'Well, it's nothing much.'

'Nussink much? Sorry. Ruining ze creative juices.'

'I just thought you could call it—'

'Go on! Zere I go again. Alvays zer chatterbox.'

'Clean.'

'Brilliant!'

'Effective.'

'Seminal.'

'Fluid.'

They flocked to shake his hand, welcome him to the group and introduce him to its activities, which covered everything: home affairs, media, fashion and design, technology and communication. They got to work on the new brand name immediately. Erikson shouted the orders.

'Christian, go and notify the Mainframe of our new addition to the group. The rest of you, let's have some bright ideas.'

There was a long pause.

'You've tampered with my plans once too often, Velcro, and now you must pay the price.'

'Leave him alone!'

'Ah, my beauty. Your concern for this man is touching. Do not worry. We shall find a safe place for him on the moon.'

'But there *are* no safe places on the moon.'

'Oh dear. What a pity.'

'Don't think you have won, doctor. You can't change people's attitudes that easily.'

'Agate, my darling. Reverse the polarity of the pleasure-beam.'

'But that will turn them into zombies. Honestly! Help me! It's our only chance!'

Edward flicked the channels of his watchman. The train gathered speed.

'Hi. Welcome again to *Consumer Watchdog*. Tonight: Summer Swimwear – Beauty or Beast? Mattresses that could cost you more than a good night's sleep, and forty new ways of spending that extra money. But first—'

Edward switched it off and stared out into the night.

'HAVE YOU HUGGED YOUR HATCHBACK?' inquired a billboard.

Edward didn't feel like hugging anyone. Since his auspicious debut at Bright Ideas, the day had deteriorated rapidly. After work he had been forced to wait for the damage caused to his flat to be processed at Fetcher Damage Control. Under the universal insurance scheme the Environment was pledged to rectify all damage caused by Fetchers. The waiting room was crowded with harassed owner-plaintiffs and their miscreant Fetchers. It was like a crèche from a futuristic horror film. The interview had gone badly. When the Fetcher started to tell its side of the story, he lost his rag and kicked it a number of times. This behaviour backfired and Edward had to agree to attend a Fetcher-Owner Reconciliation Course before the repairs would be paid for. Already that afternoon he had had to listen to talk of 'personal space', 'angry feelings' and 'vibrations', whilst the Fetcher gloated over his painful apprenticeship in personal relationships.

When he returned to Sophie's flat, she had left him a note on the TV. He pressed the PLAY button and she appeared wearing a hideous early eighties ra-ra.

'Edward. Where have you been? We're off to the party. We'll meet you there.'

Charles was hovering in the background looking positively daemonic. After all they had been through in the last couple of days, and especially last night, he had expected her to wait for him. Perhaps it had been no more than a casual fling that was all over now. Without professional counselling it was impossible to tell. He sat nursing his pride. On the seat next to him a young mum sat nursing a baby. He kept his attention on the window to avoid the spectacle.

On a passing billboard was a picture of an enormous shopping centre that dwarfed the one he had seen in Sellingfield. Another poster rolled into view, depicting a healthy young couple on a shopping buggy that was loaded to the brim.

'CHOICE IS FREEDOM'

read the slogan. Hadn't they condemned the Sellingfield Project? Surely that included Megamarkets. It all made no sense unless the Sellingfield Project and its overthrow had been an enormous con. But surely the press would have found out and exposed it. The train stopped. Battersea Park. Edward got out. The power station was awash with light. He could just make out the rollercoaster thundering between the chimneys.

Leaving the station behind him, he turned the corner of a street and came into the road where the party was being held. She sprang from behind a low hedge.

'Hi. I'd *love* to hear your opinion on a great new fragrance for men. PENETRATOR. Have a free sample.' She drenched him. 'How do you feel?'

'Wet.'

The girl looked confused. 'We don't have that on the response sheet.'

'Smelly.'

'No. Not that, either.'

'What *do* you have?'

'Debonair, chic, elegant, sophisticated or *macho*?'

'Elegant.'

'Oh. Not *macho*?'

'All right. Macho.'

'Oh. Well done. That's the answer that entitles you to—'

Edward dodged past her and sprinted the remaining

yards to the party house. The door was already being opened for a young couple. He followed them in as the host was admiring their costumes.

'Oh, that is true punk, Jamie.'

'No, actually it's Duran Duran. Remember them?'

'No.'

'Well, neither do I really. I borrowed this lot from my uncle.'

'Wow, Venetia. You look like a set of lagged pipes. Authentic aerobics. How did you get that cellulite effect on your thighs?'

'It's not an effect,' said Jamie.

'Only joking, only joking. Well, go on through. The food's over there, the music's over there, and Christ, someone's been sick over there.' The host inspected Edward. 'Hi,' he said guardedly. Edward's clothes could never be attributed to any era of fashion.

'Edward Wilson. Friend of Sophie's.'

'Oh, right. Come in.'

'Where shall I put my coat?'

'Oh. Just chuck it on the floor.'

The host turned away and put his arm round a girl who had been hovering nearby. Edward edged into the flow of people orbiting the dance-floor. He cast his eyes around for Sophie, but couldn't see much in the flashing lights. Someone dug him in the ribs.

'Don't tell me. You're the token gate-crasher. Right?'

Edward humoured the insult as the drunk laughed generously. He tried to detach himself and resume the hunt for Sophie.

On the dance-floor Charles and Sophie were smooching to the eighties hit 'Bright Eyes'. Charles was trying to nibble her earlobe.

'Charles. Don't.'

'But why Edward, of all people?'

'*You* went off the Pill.'

'Sophie. I was putting on weight.'

She slapped his hand away from her bottom.

'Anyway, Edward did very well in Sellingfield.'

'He had no idea what he was doing. If it wasn't for me he'd still be sitting in his office. And all so you could get that superdooper leak.'

'And I've said thank you.'

'Say it again.' He attempted crude docking manoeuvres. She wriggled deliciously.

On the edge of the dance-floor, Edward caught a glimpse of Charles and Sophie heading for the bar. He lurched through the crowd to reach them.

'Sophie.' He gripped her elbow. She turned.

'Oh, there you are. Why were you so late getting back? I hate people being late.'

Edward's reserves of righteous indignation evaporated. 'Sorry.'

'You're forgiven. Who's this?' Oscillating behind him was the drunk, who, after his opening insult, had adopted Edward as his friend, companion, soulmate and crony.

'Oh. This is . . .'

'Patrick. Ooooh Garrrrd, she's beautiful, mate. Hold this.' He dropped his can of wine on Edward's foot and lunged at Sophie, missed and clasped at Edward's legs for support.

'Are you OK with him?' asked Sophie.

'I was going to ask you the same question,' said Edward, glaring at Charles.

'Hi, Edward,' said Charles, grinning as Patrick clawed his way into the upright position. 'How's Flexispace?' There was more than a hint of *Schadenfreude* in his tone. 'Keeping you busy?'

'Actually, I'm in the Bright Ideas Department.'

Charles fell silent.

'Gosh, that sounds exciting. I can't wait to hear all about it,' said Sophie, genuinely intrigued. Patrick tightened his arm around Edward's shoulders.

'You leave us alone,' he said, jutting his chin at Sophie.

'Come on, Edward. Let's get some more booze. He held Edward like a vice and steered him towards the bar, leering back at Sophie. 'I'll see *you* later, darling.'

'Well, Sophie. Looks as if he's left you for another man,' said Charles, handing her a can of wine.

'What was that you said about Flexispace? I've never heard of it.'

'Oh, it's nothing.' He took her hand. There was another slow one playing. Never mind, thought Charles. The Main-frame will think of something . . .

The music ceased. In its place someone had tuned in to the chimes of Big Ben. Midnight. It was Difficult Day. Outside, a fleet of vans, their amber lights flashing, raced to block the street exits. Uniformed squads leapt from the rear doors, their metalled boots hammering on the road. They carried long, thin sticks and tall Perspex riot shields. A window-pane shattered. Then another.

'Tear-gas!' screamed someone, as oily white smoke bil-lowed into the room. Outside, a loudspeaker crackled into life.

'Come out with your hands up. You are all under arrest.'

4
PROGRESS IS POWER

Edward stood outside facing the wall with Charles, Sophie and Patrick in a long line of drunken partygoers. The Difficult Day police swaggered along the line with their uniforms and colour-coordinated matching riot shields and sticks, determined to get as much as they could out of their annual day of irresponsible power. The row of flashing vans formed a tight cordon. Escape from the garish advertisements emblazoned on the sides was impossible. The loudspeaker was barking the old Riot Act that had been invoked during the Difficulties. Two spotlights criss-crossed the line of offenders. Edward told Charles he felt sick.

'Who said that?' snapped a volunteer.

'*He* did,' squealed Charles.

The volunteer thwacked Edward across the kidneys and strolled along the line-up in a state of ill-concealed joy.

'There's always some idiot who won't keep his mouth shut,' gloated Charles.

'Who was that?' spat another volunteer, whirling on her heel.

Charles pointed at Edward. 'It was him – aaaaaahhhh gggggg!'

The volunteer strutted on, jauntily cradling her riot stick as Charles checked the damage to his shoulder.

'Right, you lot,' crackled the loudspeaker. 'You've all been found to be in breach of the Emergency Powers Act. You are all under arrest. We've got your names and addresses, and you're all very, very guilty. Right. Now clear off . . . Oh, and thanks for being such good sports. The boys and girls appreciate it.'

The volunteers drummed a hearty applause on their riot shields and jogged off to the vans, eager for more action.

Edward felt as any lovesick drunk would feel with a bruised kidney, a poor relationship with his Fetcher and a growing awareness that life wasn't all it was cracked up to be. Difficult Day was all right as far as it went – as a reminder of the bad old days before the Environment, but somehow . . .

The party dispersed into the night.

'Right. Let's go eat,' proposed Charles.

'Nothing else to do, I suppose,' shrugged Edward.

'Marvellous idea,' purred Sophie. 'Let's go to Schrinks.'

Schrinks was an outlet of the Theme Burger Chain. Its low, round doorway and bulbous portals were obscenely Freudian to those inclined to think that way. Above the door was a sign: BACK ENTRANCE. Inside, loosely arranged groups of psychiatrists' couches nestled in a dense forest of rubber plants. Waiters in thick suits and white coats wrote orders on notepads and frowned. Viennese waltzes wafted from the recessed simulated oak panelling, which was adorned with Victorian daguerrotypes and framed Rorschach ink-blots. The waiters' rollerskates were the only concession to normality.

'Welcome to Schrinks,' said a young bespectacled waiter, trying hard to sound avuncular. Around him, Charles, Edward and Sophie were appreciating the effects of drink, tiredness and injury on the soft couches. 'I'm Dr Simon. I'm your consultant for this morning's eating experience. Please feel free to tell me your innermost desires.'

Edward scanned the menu. 'I'm having a Nervous Breakdown.'

Dr Simon looked concerned. 'Major or minor?'

'Major. And a coffee-style drink.'

'Warm or cold?'

'Warm, please.'

'Mmmmm,' murmured Dr Simon significantly, writing

a long note on his pad. Sophie felt like a small Anxiety Attack with a side of Fries. Charles was having a Delusion of Grandeur.

'Large, or extra-large?' probed Dr Simon.

'Just a small one. What's that served with?'

'Bite-Sized Pillows of Paranoia with optional Guilt on the side.'

'OK. Hold the Guilt.'

'That's OK. But what would your mother say if she knew you weren't eating up the Guilt?'

Charles laughed at that one.

'Please relax. There's no need to be nervous,' Dr Simon soothed, killing Charles' laughter instantly. 'The nice nurse will soon be along with your disorders.'

Schrinks had become the most successful burger chain in the Environment, since it was genuinely relaxing to eat there and there was no charge for the food. Clients paid a consultation fee by the minute and ate as much as they liked. This encouraged fast turnover and high profits.

It was going to be a long session, and to hell with the cost. Charles, Edward and Sophie had made a very good start to Difficult Day. On the way to Schrinks they had been arrested twice, detained once, and gone through four stop-and-searches, a road-block, and a hilarious identification parade in party masks. Sophie in particular found Charles' performance hysterically funny.

Edward frowned on his couch, toying absentmindedly with a phallic peppergrinder until he realized what he was doing (and that the waiter was taking notes) and put it down on the low table with affected nonchalance. In stormed Uncle Ziggy, the Schrinks father-figure himself. A cheer rose from the scattered diners.

'Sank you. Sank you! I hope you're all haffink a goot time! Now zen.' He produced a long plastic container. 'Please don't be ashamed. But who ordered ze Penis Envy Hot Dog?'

A man in the far corner owned up.

'Ah. So. Zere iss no cause for embarrassment. Do you vant to talk about it?'

'No. Erm. I want to eat it.'

'You vanna *eat* it? Let's go into my study and talk about it first.'

The early morning diners laughed heartily as the blushing man was led away.

Edward was learning to hate these petty acts of human degradation that passed for entertainment. It reminded him of the alternative cabaret before the Difficulties. At least then you had the choice of not partaking, and most people didn't.

'When's the food arriving?' he asked tetchily.

'You really do have a problem, don't you?' observed the nice nurse, distributing culinary psychoses over his shoulder.

Charles whispered and Sophie snorted with laughter. She looked at her watch and gasped, spraying her couch liberally with Anxiety Attack. 'Turn the TV on, Charles.'

Charles pressed the button on the tabletop. It showed an aerial picture of Trafalgar Square. A commentator's head shot up from the manhole cover in the corner of the screen with the aid of the latest video techniques, bounced into close-up, spun on its own axis like a coin and stopped dead.

'Hi. I'm Gavin. I'm your commentator for this morning's opening riot, and as you can see a record number of rioters are out this morning. Some have been waiting since the wee small hours. Marvellous carnival atmosphere, a very atmospheric occasion. We're all set to go, and don't forget, after the riot, participants can have their clothes washed clean with sub-zero temperature, biologically hyperactive Zap. Dawn.'

Dawn appeared on the horizon, a bright disc of golden light, which bounced into close-up next to Gavin. The light faded to become a female face under a mane of blonde hair.

'Hi, Gavin. Well, we've had a bit of rain this morning but not enough to dampen the spirits of this mob.'

'No, Dawn. But I'm sure the water-cannon will.'

The heads parted and left the sides of the screen, and the picture zoomed in to the other end of Whitehall. A roar broke from the crowd.

'And here come the First Company of the Environmental Order Squad, their riot shields glinting in the morning sun.'

'They'll have been up polishing those all night.'

The shields were worn like sandwich-boards, and bore the legend: POLYCARBON SHATTERPROOF FOR WINDOWS THAT LAST.

'And ha, ha, here come the vans!' chortled Gavin. The riot on the screen was nicely underway. Banners waved and paving-stones flew. The water-cannon blasted the merrymakers this way and that.

'Of course, Gavin, the water pressure is well over a hundred and twenty pounds per square inch this year, whereas . . .'

'Oh, and my word, just look at that. Ha, ha, ha, that's incredible!'

Tear-gas canisters were forming a multicoloured display. The cameras picked out rioters staggering blindly into each other and choking.

'. . . Of course there have always been some great characters involved in the riots. I can see a man down there dressed as a duck, and over there, there's a man hopping.'

'Yes. Took rather a nasty crack on the knee there.'

'Ha, ha, ha. Yes. They're all *real* characters.'

Gavin listed the companies and individuals sponsoring some of the more exhibitionist demonstrators: old favourites like millionaire philanthropist Bobby de la Banne, whose efforts in the field of egocentric bad taste had financed an entire hospital wing for the treatment of cute children with incurable diseases. Rioting of an international standard,

Dawn confirmed with some really *staggering* statistics, but was cut off in mid-gush.

The picture was now of a man on a scaffolding platform. Behind the throng of hyperactive adolescents that waved and pulled faces around him, there was a great grey building. Straining nervously under his fat arm, a scrawny young woman giggled into his microphone whenever it was held under her nose and looked as if she would run away if the fat arm would only let her. He smiled sincerely.

'Hallo, and welcome to Dungeness, for live coverage of the first power cut of Difficult Day. And the winner of Channel 12's Housey Housey Bonanza competition is gorgeous housewife Kirsty Brannett of Milton Keynes. Kirsty, love, I understand hubby is dangerously ill, so the prize money should come in especially handy.'

She tittered hysterically into the microphone.

'Well, my love, it's time to enjoy the first part of your prize soon, and we all know what that is. Kirsty is the lucky winner who's going to *press that button*! What's she going to do?' He cupped his ear at the swarm in front of him.

'Press that button!' they cried raggedly.

'Well, Kirsty? All set?'

She nodded eagerly.

'The countdown's started, so get your hand over that button. And when Kirsty hits that button, some part of the Environment selected at random will be blacked out. And that could mean you!'

The crowd chanted from ten backwards, a feat that might have been impossible without the large digital display over the presenter's head.

'Eight! Seven! . . .'

'Not yet, Kirsty . . . No. Not yet.'

'. . . Four! Three! Two! One! Press that button!'

Kirsty pressed that button, the screen went blank and all the lights in Schrinks went out. Sarcastic moans were heard in the darkness. Edward groaned sincerely.

'I'm going for a walk,' he said, in the general direction

of Charles and Sophie. But Sophie was shrieking and laughing at something Charles was doing to her in the darkness and didn't hear.

Edward groped his way out of the door and skulked off into the cold morning air to Hyde Park, where he sat down on a bench to ease his throbbing head and settle his rebellious stomach. The major Nervous Breakdown was feuding with something horrible he must have drunk at the party with Patrick. Listening to the riot in the distance, he came to realize something he must have known all along. He hated the bloody Environment and always had done. He hated it more and more every day. It was bloody stupid, bloody silly and bloody dishonest. And that bloody Charles and that bloody Sophie bloody loved it. Bloody idiots.

Above the riots, the road-block and barricades, the burning and looting and slogan daubing, above the television cameras and the roof of the new Megamarket construction site behind St Paul's, above Hyde Park, a Skysmile Helicopter pilot was scanning the ground on his monitor. His job was to make sure everybody was having a good time and arrange, for anyone who wasn't, that amusement would come their way fast. Today, with the festivities engaging the hearts and minds of the Environment, his job was an easy one. The centres of fun were clearly defined. All he had to do was scan the outskirts and act as sweeper for anyone who was missing out.

This one in Sector C stood out like a gangrenous thumb. He zoomed his camera on to the subject and sent the image off with a flick of a switch to the Mainframe. It identified the subject as Edward Wilson, diagnosed unjustified girlfriend worries combined with a hangover, and recommended ground support. The pilot picked up his transceiver and got through to Wilf, who was covering the park.

Wilf acknowledged, took a swig from a bottle, coughed, spat, shoved a hand into the pocket of his filthy overcoat, rubbed his stubbly chin with the other and shuffled off to Sector C.

Edward was glowering levelly across the bloody Serpentine, when a dirty brown object sat down next to him and coughed disgustingly.

''Allo, guvnor. You on yer own, then?'

'No,' said Edward. 'I'm holding a cocktail party.'

'Not many turned up yet.'

'That's because I didn't invite anyone,' said Edward. 'I didn't invite you, either.'

'Oh, I expect the others'll be along later.'

Edward fired a savage glance at Wilf's dishevelled features. 'Why don't you just go away.'

'Pardon? Have you got something for a cup of tea? I take all the major credit cards.'

'I haven't got any money,' lied Edward.

'It's a hard life being a dosser,' affirmed Wilf sympathetically. 'You look pretty low yourself.'

'That's none of your business.'

'What's none of my business?'

.'*My* business.'

'Oh, that. D'yer do a job, then?'

'Yes,' growled Edward, rising. 'As a matter of fact, I do. And I think I'll go there now.' He stumped off across the gravel, feeling angry at not having had the courage to shove the nosy bugger into the Serpentine and silly for claiming he had a job to go to on a national holiday. But it might not be such a bad idea. It might even be quiet today.

It wasn't. The Bright Ideas Department was in full emergency session. The relaunch of Kotzenbrau beer had been an overnight disaster. As Edward was making his way to the Environment Building, Dr Erikson was already addressing the committee.

'Zo. How do ve improve ze product?'

The committee knew this one by heart. 'Change the slogan,' they chanted.

The original slogan had been dreamt up while Edward was away at a Fetcher-Owner Conciliation meeting. Billboards and TV commercials announced the slogan in bold

letters: KOTZENBRAU ... IT'S TOO GOOD TO
DRINK. The public appeared to have taken it literally.
The real problem, though, was the product itself. A survey
revealed that seventy-three per cent hated the taste and the
other twenty-seven per cent hated the aftertaste. Two top
marketing experts had been invited to explain the problem.
The first saw it in terms of zones: Zone A was London and
Zone B was everywhere else.

'. . . and both zones hated it,' he concluded triumph-
antly.

The second pundit explained they needed to target the
C3s without alienating the A4s or dismissing the E2s. What
was needed was upmarket imaging, high-profile packaging
and huge financial carroting. He suggested a big, busty
actress caressing a bag of Kotzenbrau suggestively and
saying 'Kotzenbrau . . . with free cash bonanza competition.
Mmmmm!'

It was at this point that Edward loped in looking for
somewhere quiet and dark to feel sick in. Dr Erikson
greeted him warmly, if a little too loudly.

'Take a seat, Vilson. Can you sink off *vun* thing zet can
be said for trinking Kotzenbrau?'

Edward's stomach rose up in revolt at the mention of its
worst enemy. He sat down to quell it. That must have been
the stuff he was drinking last night.

'Vell, Vilson? Zere must be somesink zet can be said for
trinking the stuff?'

'Yes,' retorted Edward. 'It makes you drunk.'

'Brilliant! "It Makes You Drunk!" Forget ze busty
actress. Ve'll show somevun completely out off his skull!
Vilson, you're a chenius!'

The committee buzzed with excited approval. A campaign was hurriedly mapped out and transferred to the
Mainframe for immediate execution, and the committee
dispersed to get back to the joys of Difficult Day.
Dr Erikson clapped Edward on the back as Spung
hopped around Edward like an enraptured frog, croaking:

'Kotzenbrau ... It makes you drunk! Kotzenbrau ... It makes you drunk!'

Dr Erikson joined in the chorus and both danced out into the corridor. There was a selection of easy chairs around the edge of the committee room. Edward found the easiest one and fell asleep.

Sophie had been trying to find Edward all afternoon. She had called him at home, but found only his forlorn Fetcher, who had learned to love Edward at the Fetcher-Owner Conciliation meeting and was missing him dreadfully. It had been impossible to find him on any of the work extensions because the switchboard staff were staging a sit-in and were too drunk to do anything but sing. It was the only time of year for people to sing songs of revolution without fear of appearing old-fashioned. Sophie arrived at the Environment Building to look for herself. To lose two of her closest male associates on the one day of the year when sociability was at a premium was really too bad. She asked the lift for the Bright Ideas Department, thirty-eighth basement level. But a power cut earlier in the day had wiped its memory and in the throes of an identity crisis it whizzed up and down the building, opening its doors at random and shouting 'What am I?' to the empty corridors.

Eventually the laws of chance brought her to the thirty-eighth basement level and she jumped out. 'What am I?' called the lift.

'I suppose you must be an unidentified flying object,' muttered Sophie as she strode off down the corridor. Happy at last, the lift shot upwards and smashed itself to pieces against the Environment Building's roof.

Edward woke up to find Sophie tugging at his shirt.

'Wake up, Edward, I've been looking for you everywhere. You've got to come with me. Charles has had an accident.'

'Good. That's the best news I've heard all day.'

'It's not funny.'

'I'm not laughing.'

'He's broken both his legs.'

'Hahahahahaha!'

'I told you, it's not funny. He was jumping up and down on the roof of a police van, and it drove off.'

'Hahahahahahaha!'

'Let's go to the hospital . . . I thought maybe we could have dinner at my house afterwards.'

'OK. But let's have dinner first and go in the morning. It *is* Difficult Day.'

'You're jealous of him, aren't you?'

'Yes,' confessed Edward.

'There's no need. Really.' She kissed him.

'Really?'

'Really.'

'OK, we'll go and see Charles some time next week, then.'

'Promise?'

'Promise.'

Charles was having a great time in hospital. He had a private room with a TV, and constant attention from a bewildering number of beautiful nurses. In the first twenty-four hours he had arranged several promising lunch-dates. Nowadays a simple fracture could be healed in practically no time, and the painkillers induced a euphoria that made him putty in the hands of the doctors who offered him a wide variety of shady deals under the aegis of the pharmaceutical industry. They showed him countless promotion videos for wonderful drugs that were mixed into Cordon Bleu meals and vintage wines. He had narrowed them down to a short list of two. With a complete course of Diazaphit à la Nouvelle Cuisine came a chance to win a timeshare in the Bahamas, but the side-effects he saw on the video rather outweighed the lure of the Caribbean. He declined graciously, much to the annoyance of the doctor, who only needed to foist this dangerous drug on one more unfortunate to win a world cruise.

Instead, Charles opted for a course of Châteaubriand impregnated with Atrogen, whose only side-effect was an aphrodisiac surge that coincided nicely with the half-hourly visits of the delectable nursing staff. Underneath it all, Charles was a randy, sexist little shit, and he was proud of it. He hardly even cared that Sophie never paid him a visit during his convalescence. He could always pick up with her when he got out. There was so much to keep him amused and happy. There were the fabulous nurses, video games, *tai chi* physiotherapy, TV. The news kept up to date with all the Environmental developments, such as the grand opening of the London Megamarket, and of course there were all the adverts to amuse him.

Was it the drugs, or were the adverts getting even better? That one for Kotzenbrau was so good, he ordered an enormous binliner-sized bag of it, as did seventy-three per cent of the population, and lay in euphoric drunkenness until the sad day of his discharge, when he returned to work and discovered that Edward was enjoying no small amount of kudos within the Department as the creator of the new Kotzenbrau image, one which had made it the leading brand overnight despite its disgusting taste. And Sophie must have been watching Edward every minute of the day. She was impossible to find.

Even Sir Desmond was impossible to find. The old Dartmouth charm could extract nothing from his receptionist. She insisted she had no idea where the elderly knight had gone, and no idea when he would be back.

Sir Desmond was on the top floor of the building preparing for a meeting with *him*. In the reception room, he was cowering in a reclining chair, the secretary astride him. His eyes were watering with pain.

'Now, lie still, Sir Desmond. This has to be done. Otherwise *he* won't see you.'

'But, please hurry. I *must* report to *him*. Aaaah!'

'Sorry. Did that hurt? Just a few more, Sir Desmond. Head back.'

'Is this really necessary?' he pleaded.

'I'm afraid we can't have a single nostril hair showing. *He* can't stand the sight of them. It's been nostril hairs all week, I'm afraid,' sighed the secretary. 'I don't know how much more of this I can take, really I don't.'

'Aaaagh! I have to see *him* about that Wilson chap. He's . . . aaaghh! . . . outgrown Bright Ideas already. Aaagghh!'

'There.' She brushed the loose hairs from her hands, lit up a cigarette and dismounted wearily. 'Nothing to offend *him* now. Drink?' She poured out a large Scotch.

'It's a little early for me. What about paperclips?'

'I haven't tried those.'

'No. Paperclips and *him*.'

'Paperclips are *his* friends this week,' she explained like a tired schoolmistress. Sir Desmond wondered who was humouring whom. 'Oh. And *he* started lisping this morning.'

'Lisping? That's a new one.'

'Yes.' She inhaled deeply. 'Rather badly, I'm afraid. *He*'d probably appreciate it if you lisp as well. And er . . .'

'My shoes?'

'No. Your watch. Leave it with me. It's ticking.'

The intercom buzzed. Sir Desmond suffered a familiar shrinking of the digestive system. It was time.

He passed through the silent antechamber, ticking off a mental checklist of dos and don'ts, and entered softly. *He* was lying at the far end of the room, gazing up through the long window. Sir Desmond approached with caution, lest he startle *him*, when, without taking *his* eyes from the window, *he* spoke in *his* thin, high voice.

'I have been watching the pigeonth. They fly well. Tell me, how are the Megamarketh progrething?'

'Well, er . . . We've opened nearly all of them now. We're thtill monitoring intake, but theventy-three per thent of the conthuming Environment thpend eight hourth or more a day making their thelectionth on them.'

He turned sharply and focused *his* good eye on Sir

Desmond. 'Thir Desmond, my naughty cat'thpaw. Why are you lithping?'

Sir Desmond flushed and looked at his feet. A thousand terrible consequences filled his mind. 'Sorry. How silly of me.'

He returned his attention to the pigeons. 'No, no. Continue. It amutheth me. Governing the Environment ath I do, I theldom have time for dithractionth. Ah ... time, time. Too little time. How I loathe to hear a ticking watch. A ticking watch remindth me of Death, Old Father Death, Thir Desmond ...'

'Er, yeth.'

'Look down through the window with me. Ith all London not now therved by jutht one Megamarket holding a permanent clothing-down thale at unbeatable pritheth?'

Sir Desmond peered on to the Megamarket below. 'Yeth. Ten thquare mileth all under one roof.'

'It ith a fine lithp you have, my cheeky turnthpit. Generally I hate lithpth. But yourth ith thomehow ... pure.'

'Thank you,' said Sir Desmond uneasily.

'Did I appear in any advertithmenth thith week? Wath I thmiling?'

'Yeth. The one where you are athleep on a thofa with your thumb in the air, dreaming of extra interetht.'

His face became suddenly older and frailer. 'Only *one* advertithment? Ha, it ith fitting. I am thurpluth to requirementh. Thoon I shall return to the farm.'

'Ah. The farm. Yeth. The farm.'

Sir Desmond was relatively sure of himself when discussing the farm. 'Lincolnshire.'

'Don't tell me. Top right?'

'Approthimately.'

'Doth it prothper?'

'Egg yield ith up by two and a half million.'

'Come, come. Don't bore me with detailth. Whoth idea wath that ridiculouth thlogan for beer?'

Sir Desmond was suddenly reminded of the purpose of

his visit. 'Ah, yeth. Edward Wilthon. I wanted to athk you . . .'

'Ah. Our little protégé. Give him enough cable and he may electrocute himthelf. But then again, he might not. Keep them following him.'

'You mean Charleth and Thophie?'

'Ethpecially them. And have hith Fetcher programmed for thurveillanth.'

'I've already done that.'

'Thtill. Enough work. I have dreamt well thith week. Let me show you Phathe Three.'

He pressed a button on the floor beside *him* with a bony finger, and the wall facing the window became a cinemascope-sized screen. The windows dimmed like huge sensitive sunglasses, and Sir Desmond gasped in humble wonderment at the vision of the future which appeared before him.

'Behold.' *His* voice quivered in awe of *his* creation. 'The Environment in itth completion. The latht vethtigeth of the old world gone.'

'When will thith be?' pleaded Sir Desmond in ecstasy.

'Thoon.'

Sir Desmond savoured his first glimpse of the sociologists' El Dorado, a dream that once seen would consume its beholder with an inferno of hope and idealism, a wonderland so exquisitely perfect that it would be grossly irresponsible to broadcast its exact form to the world. To know such perfection without the potential to realize it instantly would lead only to frustration and misery. It is better and wiser merely to allude obliquely to what Sir Desmond witnessed that afternoon in 1994 on the wall of the office of the top floor of the Environment Building in London, and leave it at that.

'Thir Dethmond?'

Sir Desmond was on his knees, mouthing silent words of wonder.

'Thir Dethmond!'

'Yeth . . .' he whispered dreamily.

'Help me to thtand up. I have been lying here naked for three dayth, and my bum ith killing me.'

Edward wasn't enjoying his cult status one little bit. He insisted to everyone that the famous slogan had slipped off the top of his head. It had been an accident. He hated Kotzenbrau and despised the commercial. But these pro-testations brought ripples of laughter from the Bright Ideas Department. To them he had become a guru, and his most off-hand utterances were treated as rare gems of wisdom. Even Sophie developed a wide-eyed awe in his presence. And she was never out of his presence these days, it seemed. His Fetcher, too, was having a deep abiding crush on him and worshipped him as a god. The only escape from either of them was when he held court in the Bright Ideas Department. And their contemptible sycophancy was beyond endurance.

The morning after Sir Desmond's apocalyptic vision, Dr Erikson presented a new problem to Bright Ideas.

'Ladies and gentlemen. Ze Mainframe hass chust come up wiz a new problem for us. Ve need a new campaign for "Plush Luxury Four-Ply Toilet Paper". Ze current slogan, "Enjoy your tender moments viz Plush" isn't working. Ve need somesink zat packs a liddle more punch. Any suchestions?'

All eyes turned to Edward, who rolled his own upwards in exasperation. Did it really matter, all this? Someone suggested slow-motion footage of puppy dogs playing in a pile of it, but was ignored.

'How about some funny shots of babies, dressed up in it?' offered another. This was laughed at. Spung suggested using 'It makes you drunk' since it had a proven track record. The committee pretended not to hear.

'How about this . . .' proposed an eager new recruit. 'An exciting action film of a tough guy on a boat winding in a roll of it with a barracuda hooked on the end . . .?' Unanimous derision.

'Vell? Any ideas, Edward?'

Edward sighed at his dull disciples. 'Well. We all know what toilet paper's for, don't we?'

'What is it for?' asked Spung.

'For wiping your bottom.'

Dr Erikson was ecstatic. 'It's so simple it's beautiful. I hear music! *The Birds*, by Respighi. A flushing of water, a toilet door opens. A beautiful woman emerges and says: "Plush Luxury Four-Ply, For Wiping Your Bottom." Vilson! You are a chenius!'

And íf the resulting sales figures were anything to go by, Dr Erikson was right. Within a week, seventy-three per cent of the Environment was wiping its bottom with Plush Luxury Four-Ply. Edward was set to become a personality.

Sir Desmond stopped trying to get the computer to do his bidding. He put a call through to Charles to ask him to come and help out. Charles bounced in. The Château-briand impregnated with Atrogen had more than healed his fractured legs. It had improved them. He was enjoying the use of his legs like a three-year-old. Charles enjoyed *everything* like a three-year-old. He had the three-year-old's capacity to live for the moment. It didn't matter to him that he hadn't seen Sophie since Difficult Day when he was lying on Oxford Street taking bids from rival ambulances. Far from it. Sir Desmond was worrying him, though. He always had a glazed look in his eye when trying to tackle a computer, particularly after lunch, but there was something just short of sinister in the trancelike expression that Sir Desmond had kept lapsing into of late.

'Is anything the matter, Sir Desmond?' he inquired.

'What? Oh. No. I mean, yes. The Mainframe. I can't er . . .'

'Leave it to me, Sir Desmond.' His hands clattered deftly over the keys. 'Is it by any chance about that chap Wilson?'

'As a matter of fact, yes. Have you seen that Plush advertisement?'

Charles frowned. 'Yes. Brilliant, isn't it? Ah. Here we are.'

They examined the prognosis on the screen. The frown lifted from Charles' face and landed on Sir Desmond's.

'Ah, well, Charles. Better get him in here, I suppose. About time I met him face to face.'

Charles tapped out Edward's home number and Sophie appeared on the screen.

'Oh. Hallo, Charles,' she said, breezily. 'How're your legs?'

Charles' lips tightened involuntarily. 'Fine. Just tell the boy wonder that Sir Desmond would like to see him *now* in his office, will you?' He tapped out another number and cancelled lunch with a nurse who had no intention of turning up, anyway. He turned to Sir Desmond. 'He should be along soon, Sir Desmond . . . Sir Desmond?'

But Sir Desmond had apparently been mesmerized by a paperclip that he was turning slowly in his hands. Charles picked up a consumer magazine disc and put it in the slot.

Three hours later, Edward sauntered into Sir Desmond's office and said Hi.

'You took your time, didn't you?' blustered Charles. 'Sir Desmond is a busy man.'

Sir Desmond looked up from his paperclip absently and blinked. 'Ah. How do you do? You must be Wilson. I'm Sir Desmond Riley, Head of . . . Head of . . . Do sit down. Now, obviously I don't know anything about you, but Charles here says you're wasted in the Bright Ideas Department.'

Charles gave Edward a conspiratorial wink.

'So,' continued Sir Desmond. 'How do you fancy a change?'

'Well, I . . .'

'Excellent. Well, I think there's only one choice for you.

We'll fix it up for you to appear before *The Firing Squad* tonight.'

Sir Desmond arranged to meet Sophie and Charles at Ninth Thermidor, a little French place he knew, so they could watch *The Firing Squad* on TV and enjoy a good meal at the same time. It was a strained occasion for all concerned. Sophie was too worried for Edward's sake to talk, and Charles, for some reason, didn't have much to say to Sophie. Sir Desmond kept slipping into narcolepsy and had to be bump-started at the beginning of each course. Even the little Fetcher failed to charm them, falling over with trays of Poulet à la Broche and crying 'Oh merde. Je suis tombé!'

Charles ordered coffee and switched on the screen. The following is a transcript of the programme, copyright Environment Channel 16 Current Affairs Dept, 1994:

(MARTIAL THEME MUSIC)
SERGEANT MAJOR: Ready! Aim! Fire!
(VOLLEY OF SHOTS)
CHAIRMAN: Hahahahahaha! Hallo again and welcome to *The Firing Squad*. The opportunity for you, the people who make up the Environment to question, to comment on and change the way the Environment is run. Facing *The Firing Squad* tonight we have that delightful housewife and theologian, the Bishop of Telford ...
TELFORD: Hallo!
(APPLAUSE)
CHAIRMAN: ... And steely-eyed, hard-nosed pragmatist from the Environmental Issues Discussion unit, John Marlin.
(APPLAUSE)
MARLIN: Hi.
CHAIRMAN: And lastly, but by no means leastly, haha, a newcomer to the programme, a warm welcome please for the Environmental Creative Policies spokesman: Edward Wilson.
(APPLAUSE)
WILSON: Hallo.
CHAIRMAN: And we'll be back after this ...
(GET UP 'N' GO SIGNATURE TUNE)

MARY: Coffee, Susan?

SUSAN: Mmm. OK (THINKS) Eulgh! Decaffeinated coffee. Taste so bitter and doesn't even wake me up . . . Mary, have you tried this?

MARY: What's that?

SUSAN: It's new. It's called Get Up 'N' Go – instant decoffee-nated caffeine.

MARY: Mmmmmm!

SUSAN: Yes. All the buzz of caffeine without that nasty coffee taste.

BOTH: Mmmmmmmmmm!

SUSAN: Come on, Mary. We've got lots to do! Ha, ha, ha!

MAN: Why not be like Mary and Susan? Get Up 'N' Go!

CHAIRMAN: Welcome back, and our first question from our audience, carefully selected by our world-beating team of market researchers, to get a cross-section which represents you, the Environment. Our first question please. Yes.

PLANT 1: My question is this. With all the millions of pounds spent on the extravagant celebrations of Difficult Day, would it not be better spent on other, more important things?

CHAIRMAN: Bishop Telford.

TELFORD: Well. Three things you can't put a price on. They are Love, Joy and Difficult Day.

(APPLAUSE)

CHAIRMAN: John.

MARLIN: Well, with respect, Bishop, that wasn't the point of the question.

PLANT 1: Yes it was!

MARLIN: The point is this. Seventy-three per cent are in favour of it. And you can't argue with that.

(PROLONGED APPLAUSE)

CHAIRMAN: What about a comment from the audience? You there. Yes, you.

PLANT 2: Is it not the case that over three quarters of the Difficult Day budget is spent on advance publicity to persuade the public that it's a good idea?

CHAIRMAN: Edward.

WILSON: I don't see what you're complaining about. If Difficult Day's not a good idea, then how else can the Environment persuade us to think otherwise?

(LAUGHTER AND APPLAUSE)

CHAIRMAN: Next question. Come on, we haven't got all evening. Spit it out. Yes, *you*.

PLANT 3: Well, er ... Is it not the case that, what with the opening of the Megamarkets in replacement of all the shops that were looted, demolished and burnt on Difficult Day, that there's less choice now?

MARLIN: The point is this: seventy-three per cent are in favour of it, and you can't argue with that.

(APPLAUSE)

BISHOP TELFORD: Well, you know, Megamarkets are all about choice ...

(APPLAUSE)

BISHOP TELFORD: Wait a minute. I haven't finished ...

CHAIRMAN: Edward.

WILSON: Frankly, the people who make up the Environment damn well *deserve* Megamarkets.

(TUMULTUOUS APPLAUSE)

At this point, Sir Desmond had seen enough. 'What do you think, Charles?'

'I think we should go with the Mainframe on this one, Sir Desmond.'

Sophie looked from Sir Desmond to Charles questioningly. 'Well, I think Edward was magnificent. What's that got to do with the Mainframe?'

'Yes, he was, Sophie. Of course he was,' said Sir Desmond in a disturbing tone of consolation.

'I checked the Mainframe again this afternoon, Sir Desmond. It's offering Red,' said Charles enigmatically.

Sophie looked imploringly from Charles to Sir Desmond. 'He *was* funny. I liked his answers the best, didn't you?'

'I think we may as well give Red a green light, then, Charles.'

'What is going on?' begged Sophie.

Sir Desmond placed a cold hand on hers. 'Affairs of state, my dear. Affairs of state ...'

'What do you *mean*?' she pleaded.

But Sir Desmond's eyes had misted over and Charles was manically absorbed in wringing a paper napkin in his shaking hands.

5
POWER IS HAPPINESS

At the top of the Environment Building is a long, thin room. It is Room 1001. Inside this chamber *he* strode up and down, talking to the monitors and to himself. In *his* bony hands were the ads for the coming season. There was a picture of *him* dressed as a vicar cycling through a leafy Environment hamlet with *his* thumb up. The picture bore the title 'Gassability'. At the bottom was the slogan:

POWER IS HAPPINESS

He cackled. That would make the electrical people sweat. *He* perused their ad. In the electrical view of the Environment *he* stood in a kitchen next to a young woman who was lifting two baked potatoes from a microwave. The slogan read:

COME HOME TO A REAL MEAL. NUKE A SPUD TODAY

He skimmed the Megamarket promotions. Best of all was a picture of a pre-Difficulties family standing awestruck outside a Megamarket. The caption read:

THE MEGAMARKET EFFECT: IT'S BEEN HAPPENING
FOR DECADES

He turned to look at the latest bingo competition requiring his choice of winner. After all, they *were* games of chance. A bankrupt divorcee with cancer became a millionaire with a wave of *his* hand. Finally *he* scanned next week's headlines for the last time:

BILLIONAIRE GOES BANANAS ON BOOZE
BRAVE BABY BARRY BATTLES WITH NEW BRAIN

BASTARDS!
MEGAMARKET FOR MILLIONAIRES
SCANDAL OF THE SOFT TOILET TISSUE SWINDLE

And finally:

KILLER BIROS

That would keep them happy. And when the work was complete they would be happy forever. *His* cheeks were wet.

'I'm so happy,' *he* said. *His* own work was over. The tears followed the deep lines of *his* face. *His* reverie was broken by the sound of ringing. *He* stabbed at the intercom.

'Secretary-person, the bells . . . the bells . . . They've come back.' *He* wedged clenched fists against *his* ears.

'It's your telephone.'

He lifted the receiver. 'Ah. Sir Desmond, my little amanuensis. It is over.'

Sir Desmond looked surprised. He had dialled the wrong number. 'Er . . . Yes. I heard from the Mainframe this morning. Who will replace you?'

'The boy Wilson. Executive was positive. He is the one they want. I saw him on Channel 16 last night. He has wings, has he not?' Sir Desmond nodded his accord. 'It is the dawning of a New Age, Sir Desmond.' *His* monocle misted over. 'Don't cry, Sir Desmond. You'll set me off. Chin up. Think of the future, my trusty cat's paw. To the Megamarkets and to happiness. Adieu, Sir Desmond.'

He let the receiver fall, stifled a sob and pressed the intercom.

'Secretary-person, come in, would you?' *He* strolled to the window and let *his* eyes linger on the neon sign above the main Megamarket entrance.

CHOICE IS FREEDOM

it announced in letters a hundred feet high.

'You are the future,' *he* intoned. 'The beginning of the

circle. The end of an era.' *He* reached for his trusty pogo-stick and tested its spring. 'Ah. How I ache for the farm ... The little ducks and lambs calling for their mothers ...'. *He* filled *his* lungs. 'Mooooooooooooo. Mooooooooooooo.'

'You called?' The secretary stood in the doorway.

'I was calling for my mother. Secretary-person, I leave this morning. Is everything ready?'

'I have the laundry basket waiting for you.'

'Good. Well, come, come. Bring it in.' *He* turned to *his* two monitors. 'Executive. You have done everything and made everything possible. Dreamer. Dream on, beautiful Dreamer.'

The secretary wheeled in a battered and rickety laundry basket. *He* looked it over with a critical eye.

'It's a laundry basket fit for a king.' *He* lifted the lid, placed *his* hands together as if in prayer and bellyflopped into it. The secretary dropped the lid and buckled the straps. Softly from within came the strains of 'Old MacDonald Had a Farm'. The name Wilson was flashing on the terminals.

Edward and Sophie stopped at the lights to let the other shopping buggies pass at the intersection. A woman in a pink jumpsuit bounded towards them holding an opinion board. It was the fourth time in ten minutes that this had happened.

'Hi there. Can I have your opinion on the Megamarket's selectivity of colour concept?'

'I don't understand what that means ...'

'Does it make you feel awake, warm, secure or relaxed?'

'Yes,' said Edward, driving on.

'Thanks. Have a nice experience.'

Sophie was reading the paper. 'Oh, Edward. Have you seen this?

"TRANSPLANT TRAGEDY FOR TINY TOT"

Oh, doesn't she look helpless with all those wires and tubes?' For a moment Sophie looked close to tears, but brightened on turning the page.

'THE POLLSTERS SAY WE'RE PERFECT'

It was the glorious story of the family voted 'Opinion-Pollers of the Year'. There was a picture of the family surrounded by teenage girls in bikinis pouring champagne.

'They answered all the polls exactly the way the opinion poll said they should.'

Edward was taking in the video hoardings as they drove. 'Stop!' squealed Sophie. 'What's that over there?' She pointed to an enormous pink heart that throbbed fluorescently above a heart-shaped doorway whose sign read *ROMANCE WORLD* in sweeping italics. 'Oh, Edward. Let's go and have a look.' Her voice had taken on the consistency of warm marshmallow. Edward parked the buggy and they walked over to the entrance, where a smooth, deeply male voice swirled through the dry ice.

'Hi. To enter the world of romance you must first hold hands.' They clasped. 'Ah,' sighed the voice. They strolled into a world of breathtakingly bad taste: a lovers' lane of modern consumerism. 'Welcome to Romance World, where all your dreams are dreams of happiness and love. Come visit our jewellers' shops, mortgage shops and travel shops. Then rest awhile in Lovers' Meadow and pass on to the bridal shops, the His 'n' Hers shops.' The voice curdled coquettishly . . . 'and the Love Planning Booth.'

Still holding hands they drifted amongst other young couples for about half an hour until Sophie insisted they buy a selection of soft centres and join the other turtledoves lying on the astroturf by the water cascade. Edward had never in his life seen so many people cavorting. By the time they reached the meadow, Edward was suffering a surly tightening of the jaw. Sophie insisted that he pop chocolates into her mouth like all the other doting paramours. An amorous couple was frolicking in the waterfall.

'I swear to God it's the food additives that do it,' said Edward.

'Oh, Edward. Since we've arrived you've done nothing but complain about the people here. You're not being very romantic.'

'Look at them. They're like lemmings.'

Sophie had argued enough. 'Mmmmmmmm. Aren't these chocolates nice 'n' light? I wonder what our love profiles will say.' That was another thing that Sophie had insisted on. Edward scowled.

'I mean, what's the point of it all?'

'Edward. Take a look around you. It's beautiful. Hundreds of young people in love, doing what comes naturally, buying things. It's nice to see that there's still romance in a materialistic age.' She popped another choc into her mouth.

'Spare me the social comment.'

Sophie stood up. 'For God's sake, if you're going to be such a misery, I'm off.' She stamped off in a swirl of sweet-wrappings. 'I'm off to get the love profiles.'

Edward lay on his back listening to piped birdsong and low murmurings of young people in love.

'Hi!' It was a pair of plump rubber lips on a telescopic antenna that spoke. The antenna was mounted on a small tracked vehicle. The lips hovered close to his own. 'I'm Vanda. I am to be kissed.' The antenna moved the lips closer to his own.

'If you think I'm going to snog with a mobile vacuum cleaner, you're wrong.'

'Oh, come on. It's your free Kissability Test. Pucker up and give me one. And *no* tongues.' The lips made firm contact and gyrated. Edward decided that retreat was the best form of defence and backed off across the astroturf.

'Don't run away. You could win a free holiday.' Vanda's antenna extended to full height and was gaining on him. The backs of his legs came into smart contact with a low obstacle and Edward found himself sitting heavily on top of a laundry basket.

'Oh, I give up. He's too shy,' said Vanda, turning in search of another victim.

'I'm terribly sorry,' said Edward to the apparent owner of the basket.

'That's all right. Would you mind looking after it for a minute while I go and check the results of the Love Game?'

'Er, no,' said Edward. The basket stirred under him.

'Pssst! Listen!'

'What?' said Edward, jumping nervously from the source of the voice.

'I said: Pssst! Listen!'

'What are you selling?' Edward asked, eyeing the laundry basket sceptically.

'Edward Wilson—'

'How do you know my name?'

'Silence, child. And listen. I have here your Golden Keycard. Lift the lid two inches and I'll pass it to you.' From one of the corners emerged a bright gold card in a trembling bony hand. Edward took it and the lid snapped shut. He turned the card over in his hand. It was marked with a large *E* and a series of digits. He put it in his pocket. The basket resumed transmission.

'Take it to Room 1001. It's got a big, big, carpet. It's yours. The bonanza price to end all prizes. You've won the Environment.' The basket-owner returned delightedly clutching a handful of tickets. He pushed his way past Edward, who gawped in disbelief.

'Thanks, mate. I've just won the gooseberry prize in the Love Game. A holiday for three in Barbados.' The man tugged at a rope and led the battered basket away. Edward was wondering if Sophie had arranged a Practical Jokea-gram. The soft musak stopped and couples froze like children playing a party game.

A woman's voice boomed. 'This is a special announcement. Would the owner of the Golden Keycard please report to Room 1001, Environment Building.'

Sweat glistened across Edward's forehead. This was serious. He made his way to the exit.

In the entrance hall he was met by a uniformed guard, who escorted him to the lift. The lift doors opened at the top floor, where they were faced by a long blank wall. The guard removed a ring from his finger and placed it in a socket. 'Shazzam,' he commanded, and the wall slid rumbling sideways, revealing a worried-looking secretary at her desk. The wall closed behind him.

'Good morning, Mr Wilson, sir.' An uneasy grin twitched across her mouth. 'Well done. Here. Take this free Waterford cut-glass set and these vouchers for a deep-fat fryer. They come with the main prize.'

Edward took them and followed her down a corridor.

'Your Keycard, please.'

He handed her the card, which she slipped into a slit in the door. Room 1001. Edward swayed in the doorway, his breath taken away by its sheer size.

'I see what he meant about the carpet,' he whispered. The room had been stripped of any last vestige of *him* save for the carpet of irridescent yellow and red check.

'You can choose your own decor. Here's a starter disk to help you. "Interior Design for the Man at the Top".' She paused to let it all sink in. 'There's Executive and Dreamer,' she said, pointing out two monitors on the floor. 'Just call if you need me.' The door closed. Edward walked to the monitors to introduce himself.

The one called Executive began to explain its functions.

'I'm Executive and I know everything—'

'What? That's not – possible—'

Executive explained that it was, and demonstrated by obtaining an object, any object, from Edward's past. Edward chose a glass paperweight that he had once admired as a child. It had stood on a neighbour's mantelpiece. Executive located its present position and arranged to have it sent round. It proceeded to explain Wittgenstein's *Tractatus Logico-Philosophicus* and adjusted all the prices in the Mega-markets in twelve seconds flat.

'I run every aspect of the Environment for you,' it said, without appearing to boast, and simultaneously located two pfennigs that Edward had lost on a skiing holiday in Innsbruck when he was sixteen. The coins appeared on the screen. Executive converted them into a tiny replica of the Imperial Palace in Tokyo. Edward shelved further comment. Dreamer, the other monitor, was more the strong, silent type. It said its job was to dream up new ideas for Edward to choose before passing them on to Executive to carry out.

'Really? I used to do that sort of thing. I was in the Bright Ideas Department.'

'Yes. The Bright Ideas Department was one of my ideas,' said Dreamer.

Between illustrative demonstrations of their powers, the terminals explained how he was supposed to run the Environment with no previous experience. It was all terribly simple. Dreamer gave him a series of choices to make on all aspects of Environment. The one Edward chose would become the policy for the whole country.

'Now then,' said Dreamer. 'Let's have a little practice. Which new system of strategic defence?'

Various options were displayed in classic opinion-poll style.

'Er . . . B.'

'Fine. Next year's colours for men's leisurewear?'

'C.'

'Best method for disposal of toxic waste?'

'E.'

'The fifteen new things to do with cottage cheese.'

'Oh. That's a hard one . . . A, I think.'

'That's marvellous, Edward. You're a born leader,' assured Dreamer without a trace of sarcasm. 'Right. While Executive is putting your policies into operation, we might as well get on with running the shop.'

For the next two and a half hours, Edward made choices for every aspect of the country, ranging from the improbable to the unbelievable. If he showed any hint of not taking the questions seriously, Dreamer or Executive would remind him of the responsibility that comes with power, and persuade him to apply himself conscientiously once more to the task in hand. It was quite fun, really, and quite exhilarating to think of the effect these decisions might be having. For lunch, Edward chose plovers' eggs, and jokingly ordered a troupe of dancing-girls. They were still high-kicking across the room when Edward resumed the wielding of power. Already his mind was becoming hazy.

Outside in the secretary's office, his performance was proving a source of considerable interest. Sir Desmond had come up to the top floor to see how he was settling in. On the secretary's monitor, Edward could be seen striding around the room shouting orders to Executive and Dreamer whilst swigging from a can of Dom Pérignon. So little style, compared to *him*, thought Sir Desmond.

'How's he been doing?' he asked the secretary as she swallowed two Valium.

'They seem to be getting to him already. I'll tell him you're here.' She buzzed through, and Sir Desmond passed into the long antechamber.

Edward greeted him like a lost friend. 'Sir Desmond. Des. OK girls, let's wrap it up.' The dancing-girls trouped out, red-faced from their exertions. 'Can of champagne? Cigar? Like a bath?'

'Er—'

'I'll have one sent round to your office. See to it, Executive. Gold taps, the lot. What else can I do for you? Answer any questions? I'm good at that, aren't I, Dreamer?' He laughed hollowly. 'Know how the Environment works, Des?'

'Well . . .'

'Well, neither did I until this morning. These two little devils do it all. Amazing, isn't it? After the Difficulties, all the power got centralized around the Mainframe, and these two are in charge of it. And I'm in charge of them. But who's running me, that's the point, isn't it?'

'Is somebody running you?'

'Haha. No. Nobody's running me.'

'Well, there you are then. How are you getting on?' Sir Desmond took in the bare room.

'Haven't had time to furnish the place yet. Haven't had any good ideas in that sort of area. I have come up with one little idea of my own, though. Look at this. Fetcher! Come here.' A Fetcher whirred across the carpet, travelling a full sixty yards and not falling over once.

'Designed it myself. Off my own bat. Dreamer had a fit, but I've ordered Executive to put it into production. Calling it the Mark 7. Put stabilizers on the side. Can't think why nobody thought of it before.'

Sir Desmond examined the little wheels that jutted out from the Fetcher's flanks. 'Ingenious,' he attested.

'Well, leadership is a rare gift. Otherwise I'd have gift shops selling it.' He laughed uproariously at his own witticism. Sir Desmond resisted the obligation to join in. Edward's mirth subsided.

'How's Sophie?'

'I haven't seen her.'

'Oh, well when you do, send her in to see me. I'd like her to be my queen.' Sir Desmond laughed at that one, but Edward remained serious.

'What do you think of this?' He produced a paperweight from his pocket. 'Executive found it for me. The secretary brought it in with my lunch.'

It was one of those old-fashioned, cheap, snowstorm-effect ones. When shaken it made a blizzard of tiny snowflakes swirling around a snowman in a forest.

'I think it's *beautiful*,' said Edward.

'Yes, yes . . . Beautiful,' agreed Sir Desmond.

'I've always loved it.'

'Oh. Yes ... Yes. Mmmmmmmm.' Sir Desmond strained every sycophantic muscle in his body.

'Are you all right?' asked Edward. 'Look. Have it. Take it. It's a gift. If you shake it you get a snowstorm.' He tossed the revered item to Sir Desmond. 'And now I must get back to work. The Fetcher will see you out. And listen: Fetcher! Stop making that noise.' The familiar *dibidibidibi* sound made by all Fetchers ceased. Sir Desmond was aghast. Sacrilege. 'Another design improvement, Des.'

Sir Desmond closed the door quietly and returned to the secretary's office.

The meeting with Sir Desmond had created a substantial backlog: systems, layouts, additives, designs, colours ... They had all begun to blend into one. There seemed to be no end to it, but Edward set about it with gusto, the sooner to get on with the real business of improving the Environment.

Outside, Sir Desmond watched the monitor whilst the secretary sat chainsmoking.

'I don't understand it. He's not supposed to be dreaming up ideas of his own, like Fetchers that don't bloody fall over. He's supposed to make the choices from what the Mainframe has to offer. Everything he's done he's cocked up, one way or another. I never understood why the Mainframe wanted him for the job in the first place,' said Sir Desmond, shaking his head in disbelief. 'That bloody computer certainly does move in mysterious ways.'

'I'm afraid it's worse than you think, Sir Desmond,' said the secretary. 'Just before you arrived, he told Dreamer to stuff the colour selection for the new yoghurt cartons.' Sir Desmond's face whitened at the blasphemy. 'He told Executive he wants them all orange. Every single flavour. Even ... Even ...' she spluttered. 'Even Blackcurrant 'n' Country Bran. *Orange.*' It was barely a whisper. She lit another cigarette from the stub of the last. Blackcurrant 'n' Country Bran. Orange. It was too horrible to contemplate.

On the monitor, Edward was shaking his fist at Dreamer.

'Ah,' said Sir Desmond. 'It's shut down to let him cool off a bit.'

'Thank God.'

'Keep me informed of any further developments.'

The secretary crunched an empty cigarette packet and broke the Cellophane on a new one.

Inside, Edward had stopped shaking his fist.

'So you can't take the pace, eh, Dreamer? My ideas just too revolutionary for you, eh? Well, when you've got some more choices for me, let me know, won't you?' He walked to the window and looked down on London.

'How many friends have I got, Executive?'

'Nine.'

'Nine? That's ridiculous. I was the second most popular person in my year at college. There are more than nine.'

Executive checked its records soundlessly. 'I'm afraid not. Third, actually.'

'Third? Oh yes. Third. Look. There must be more than that. There's Max—'

'Max who?'

'Max Christie at college . . .'

'He's not on the list. He came off after that incident with the Saltimbocca.'

'Oh, that's pathetic. I forgave him for what he did with the starch gun. I wish I'd never brought up the subject, now. Is Sophie on your little list?'

'Off and on.'

'What do you mean?'

'Well, sometimes—'

The explanation was interrupted by the intercom. The next entertainment had arrived.

'Send them in. Executive, I want a full investigation of all my friends, starting with Charles Dartmouth.'

'Edward . . .' Dreamer was on speaking terms again.

'Oh, so you've come back.'

'I've got some more choices for you, Edward.' The

interrogation began again. Through the door streamed a dozen extremely attractive cheerleaders sporting tight sweaters decorated with a large *E*. They organized themselves into display formation, pom-poms at the ready.

'Ee-Dee-Doubleyou-Ay-Ar-Dee! Doubleyou-Eye-Ell-Ess-Oh-En! Edward Wilson, yeh-yeh-yeh!'

Edward looked up from Dreamer's screen. 'OK, girls. Not bad, but let's have it one more time, a bit more *simpatico*.' He jabbed the intercom. 'Secretary-person, get a brass band in here, would you?'

Alone in her study, the secretary let out a quiet moan. He was worse than *him*.

Charles dropped the receiver and tangoed into his bathroom. Sir Desmond had been worrying about the Mainframe again. If only he would *trust* it a bit more. The poor old man had seemed vaguer than ever, and wouldn't say what Wilson was up to. He finished brushing his teeth and gargled with Sluice; the Gateway to Fresher Breath, and poured half a bottle of Spoiler, the Aftershave for the Aerodynamic, on his face, neck, ears and torso. He looked in the mirror and rubbed his jaw.

'Charles Dartmouth, you handsome bastard,' he said. 'Little Caroline doesn't stand a chance tonight.' He flexed his muscles. 'I'm bigger than her, for a start. Still. Better wear my lucky shirt. Doo Dee Doo Doo Dee . . .'

'Doo Dee Doo Doo Dee . . .' hummed his Fetcher in another key. 'Hey, Charles. I've laid the shirt on the bed for you. Doo Doo Doo Deeeee . . .'

'Thanks, Fetch. Hey, Fetch. Come here.'

'Yes?'

'Look at my foot.'

The Fetcher looked.

'Look closely, now.'

It looked closely. Charles kicked it spinning across the room. 'Stupid little thing . . . Za za za za za . . .'

The doorbell rang to the tune of 'The Girl From Epanema'. He rumba'ed to the door. 'She's early, the little vixen. Hang on! Just making myself decent! Hope you're not . . .' He flung open the door and enveloped the female on the doorstep. After a concerted attack on the earlobes and neck, he became aware that it was not Caroline in his arms.

'Sophie.'

'Charles, I must talk to you.' Charles was blocking the door. Little Caroline could turn up at any minute.

'It's a little inconvenient at the moment, Soph.'

'Shut up and let me in.' She thrust herself past and paced into the lounge.

'Look, Soph, I'm expecting someone round . . .'

'Charles, have you seen Edward?'

'No. You don't think I'm wearing too much of this, do you?' He proffered a cheek. She gasped as Spoiler seared her lungs.

'He's not at his flat and he hasn't phoned me. What's happened to him this time?'

'Soph. Calm down, sit down, and tell me what your problem is . . .'

'I've *told* you. I can't find Edward.' Charles' fickle attention had settled on the selection of shoes that his Fetcher had laid out.

'Which shoes do you think, Soph? The big ones or the small ones?'

'*Charles*. I last saw him in Romance World—'

'That explains it, then, doesn't it? It's a wonderful place. That's where I met Caroline. Went *in* with Natasha, heh-heh.' He slipped the big shoes on. 'Mind if I watch the news? Television!'

Sophie continued. 'I'd gone to get the love profile results. We'd been arguing about some chocolates. I came back with the results – they're great, by the way, we're really made for one another – and he'd gone. Vanished. Pfff.' She clicked her fingers. 'And we had a love-potential rating of nine!' Sophie looked genuinely upset. Perfect couples often won prizes. She turned to Charles for his reaction. But he was watching the news.

'– and the Group Elected for the Rights of Microbes, or GERM, broke into an Environment Disease Research Centre over the weekend and released billions of viruses and bacteria into the surrounding countryside. They had been kept, claims a GERM spokesman, under inhuman conditions in pipettes and Petri dishes. And they say they are submitted to degrading and painful experiments. The area has now been sealed off for health reasons. And finally –' Before the presenter could reach the Snake that Eats Jam story, Sophie had turned the TV off.

'Well, Charles?'

'I was watching that.'

'I think I love him, Charles.'

Charles laughed heartily. 'Don't be ridiculous. He's an idiot.'

'Well, anyway. What should I do?'

The chimes of 'The Girl From Epanema' clanged from the hall.

'Hell. Caroline.'

'What am I going to do?'

'Hide under the bed, that's what. And don't come out until we've left.' He tried to wedge her under the futon. 'Caroline. Coming, you pretty little thing . . .' He turned back to Sophie as he glided into the hall. 'Look, I don't know where Edward is. You're a mole, ask Sir Desmond.'

The doorbell had reached 'Tall and tanned and young and lovely' as Charles opened the door.

'Caroline. What a stunning outfit.'

Sophie emerged irate and distraught, her dress awry from her confinement under the futon.

'I see,' said Caroline. 'I think I must have arrived a bit early.'

'What? Oh, for Christ's sake, Sophie. I told you to stay under the bed. Caroline, there's a simple explanation.' She didn't wait for one. She slammed the door, trapping the first twelve inches of Charles' shoe. 'Thank you very much, Sophie.' His upper half turned to glower at her, but his lower half remained fixed. He pitched forwards and backwards at the same time. Sophie screamed with laughter.

'Oh, ha bloody ha, Soph.'

Sir Desmond switched to the mid-morning news. The lead story was the ill-fated Mark 7 Fetcher that wouldn't fall over. People were demanding the old style back. Then there was the slump in the yoghurt market. There were reports of surliness to opinion-pollers and the Skysmile aircrews were having to fly in triple sorties. He turned to his Mainframe terminal and punched an inquiry to the secretary's office. Today's recipe on Channel 27 flashed up: Devilled tomatoes à la Frank Sinatra. He tried again and got through to a jacuzzi centre in Barnet. He gave up. If only he could ask Charles to help him . . . There was a knock on his office door.

'Desipoohs . . .' cooed a girlish voice from the corridor. 'It's Sophie-Wophie, your favourite little Moley-Woley. I know you've got a naughty little secret to leak to me, and I'm going to come and get it . . .' She knocked again.

Sir Desmond consulted his appointments book. Most peculiar. He didn't have a leaking session arranged for this time.

'I'm sorry, Sophie. I'm in conference.'

'Well, call an adjournment, you naughty little thing . . .'

Sir Desmond saw there would be no let-up and pressed the door button. She bounced in, wearing regulation mole attire. It was designed to make the blood pressure rocket among men of Sir Desmond's generation.

'Now, now,' quivered Sir Desmond. 'You know very well I can't possibly tell you anything. Man of my responsibility.' Over a period of time a mole and source develop a rapport, their own peculiar way of allowing official information to change hands. It was a ritual that Sophie had to a tee with Sir Desmond. She wriggled on to his lap and tickled him behind the ear.

'No, no.' The sweat was beginning to break from his forehead as she held a tantalizing finger hovering over his tummy.

'Ooh-ooh-ooh,' she teased. He began to gurgle. He was not averse to this treatment and racked his brain for some unimportant tit-bit to drop.

'Well . . . I have got a bit of a secret. Just a *little* one.'

'Oooh. Round and round the garden . . . What is it, Desipoohs?'

'More tickles first.'

'No. Leak first. Then tickles.'

'Ooowmph. All right then. The Bright Ideas Department is going to be axed. Top decision.' The horseplay ceased.

'Is that all?' Girly-Wurly became Stern Nurse.

'Yes,' said Sir Desmond, failing to notice the change of, atmosphere. 'You won't leak it to anyone, will you? Bunny-Wunny absolutely forbids it.' He wagged his index finger coquettishly.

'No. I most certainly will not.'

'What do you mean, you won't?' barked Sir Desmond, forgetting his role of Uncle Naughty.

'Where's Edward? Leak *that* to me,' she demanded.

'Let go of my ear. That really is hurting this time, Sophie.' He was trying to sound authoritarian under difficult circumstances. 'Ow. Led go ob by doze.'

She released her grip, and Stern Nurse became Lost Waif. 'Oh, *please*, Sir Desmond.' She rolled seal-pup eyes at him as he rubbed his throbbing extremities.

'No. It's classified. *I* don't even know where he is, but he's all right.'

'But why can't I—?'

'Look, you've been working too hard. I understand the Solomon Islands are rather nice at this time of the year. I'll book you two tickets for tonight's flight now.' He punched the keyboard for Environmental Airlines and got the Merchant Seamen's Crisis Line. 'Er. I'll do it later. You've got to go. That's the Environment's Pledge.' He stuck his thumb in the air. Sophie knew she was beaten. It was clear that moling was out of the question for a while.

'All right, then,' she resolved bitterly. 'The Solomon Islands it is. Five star?'

'Naturally.'

'But one thing you can be sure of: I won't enjoy it.' She removed her shoe and walloped the door-button. In a building full of automatic doors it was the nearest you could get to slamming one.

Sir Desmond tried getting through to the secretary again, and succeeded in booking tickets for *La Traviata*. Damn. He loathed opera.

Edward's relentless chiefdom of the Environment continued with no apparent sign of slacking. Dreamer was increasing the rate of questioning. Edward's brain had long since ceased to ache.

'Look at that, Executive. Another glorious sunset over the Environment,' sighed Edward.

'That's the sun *rising*, Edward.'

'It's so hard to tell nowadays . . .'

'Especially since you had the idea of making the clocks metric.'

'There's no need to be sarcastic, Executive. Just remember who's in charge. Have the men finished waterproofing the room?'

'They left half an hour ago.'

'Good.'

'Edward . . .?' It was Dreamer. 'I urgently need your attention on matters now running at top priority.'

'Well, list them as unimportant. I need time to clear my head.'

'The low-priority file is full. I must ask you—'

Edward paced the room in Bermudas and a Hawaiian shirt, firing answers in staccato bursts. The Fetcher was returning from the door, having dealt with a delivery of sand. It whirred silently across the room.

'Fetcher! Come here!'

It zipped efficiently to his side. 'Yes, Mr Wilson, sir.'

'How did you know my name?'

'Er—'

'You've been spying on me, haven't you?'

'No, Mr Wilson, sir.'

'Who were you muttering to?'

'Nobody, Mr Wilson—'

'Nobody? You were muttering to nobody?'

'Yes, Mr—'

'So you *were* muttering.'

'No M—'

'Do you dare to argue with me?' He boggled at the machine, appalled by its perfidy.

Dreamer's screen blinked urgently. 'Edward, the questions, please.'

'Just a minute, Dreamer. There's a principle involved here, and I think it's important that this Fetcher and I are able to work out the reason for its treachery and hatred in a spirit of fairness.' He wheeled on the Fetcher and kicked it with all his strength. The stabilizers held fast. 'Aghgh!' He clutched his damaged foot. 'Those bloody stabilizers.'

'Sales of the Mark 7 are close to zero,' remarked Executive.

'Oh, don't *you* start. That Fetcher's been finding out about me and my friends in secret. Did Max send you?'

'No, Mr Wilson, sir.'

'You see, Edward, people *liked* their Fetcher to fall over. It made them happy.'

'All right, Executive. You're so clever. Let's say there's a design fault and recall them all. Come on, Dreamer, think something up.'

'It wasn't my idea in the first place. Besides, I'm trying

to think up something to do with half a million tons of yoghurt in orange cartons, that are rapidly going off.'

'Change the colour of the cartons.'

'It was your idea to have them in orange.'

'Well, *I'm* in charge.'

'Yes. Could I have your selections on the following . . .'

Edward swatted the intercom. 'Secretary-person! Get me Sir Desmond Riley.'

'Immediately, sir.'

'Who said anything about immediately? Why immediately?'

'I thought—'

'Well, let me do the thinking. That's my job. Had any good yoghurt recently? I'm told it's delicious. Mmmm mmmm.'

'No, sir.'

'Try some. And send a bucket round to Sir Desmond and tell him to see me in two hours.'

Dreamer seized its chance. 'Edward—'

'Look, do you mind? I want to watch the news. It's important to keep up with current affairs, isn't it, Executive?' He looked to Executive for agreement. As a pragmatist it tended to side with Edward against Dreamer.

'Oh, let him watch the news,' it said, switching itself to Channel 48.

Garry Wayne, the boy next door with the capped teeth and tinted perm, burst into close-up.

'Hi! It's the Year of Yucky Yoghurt, say the opinion-polls, and that's official. The flavoursome range of semi-solid sourish junket has yomped the Environment's tastebuds. To blame? The recently axed foodie funsters at the Bright Ideas Department.' The news spun to a suburban front door in a leafy crescent. A surprised and dishevelled Dr Erikson appeared on the doorstep in a blaze of camera lights.

'Dr Erikson, as head of the discredited Bright Ideas Department, what is your comment on the yoghurt scandal?'

'Who are you? Leave a poor old man alone.'

'Are you denying that billions of gallons of disgusting yoghurt have been forced on to the public because of your team?'

'Whose ideas vas zis?' He turned and called. 'Spung, Spung! *Komm' doch her!* I am a poor, frail man who vas only followink orders.'

The interviewer spotted Spung. 'Is your assistant to blame?'

Erikson lunged at the camera with his cane. 'No vun vas to blame. It was 1944. I vas a young man of twenty only—'

'Dr Erikson, is it right that you personally oversaw the choice of colour for the cartons?'

'You must understand, vis ze Ardennes gone, we were fighting for our very existence. Morals ceased to mean anyzing . . .'

'Can you justify Blackcurrant and Muesli in an orange pot?'

'Justify! Ha, justify! We didn't think we needed to justify – ze Fuehrer was like a god—'

'Just tell the viewers if what you have done is fair to the Environment.'

'Fair? You talk of fair? Was Dresden fair? Was Cologne and Dusseldorf fair?' Dr Erikson slammed his door shut.

'So – Dr Erikson, the butcher of the skimmed semi-solids, as he's been dubbed, is inside and refuses to talk. This is Garren Darren, Channel 48.'

'Enough,' commanded Edward.

'Edward –' interjected Dreamer.

'Wait a minute, you meddlesome micro. Executive, is the room ready?'

Executive confirmed that it was.

'Right. Open the tanks. Dive, dive, dive. Right, let's get this over with, shall we, Dreamer?' Dreamer was only too pleased. The sooner the better.

Several thousand nautical miles from Room 1001, the sun was beating down on the naked body of one Environment mole on official rest leave. It scorched the fine white sand around the coconut matting on which she lay.

With her fingertips she stroked a muscular thigh that rested against her own. 'Oh, Charles. I *am* enjoying this. Glad you came?' Charles was pleased about everything except the insect that had just bitten him.

'Yeah. Great idea to get away from it all. You needed a holiday.'

'*I'm* glad you came.'

He squinted at her salmon-pink skin. 'Careful, Soph. You're burning. Let me rub some oil in.' He squelched away with a bottle of Factor 7 and continued long after the bottle was empty and the coverage complete.

'Mmmmmm. That feels good,' she crooned.

'And what about the oil?' The obligatory, toe-curling quip from Charles. 'Another fruit punch?'

'Mmmmmmmm. Yes, please. Oh, I do like to be beside the seaside.'

'Oh, I do like to be beside the seaside!' sang Edward at precisely the same moment, sploshing about the room in four inches of warm water. About him a flotilla of toy boats and plastic ducks floated, whilst the monitors rested on the sandy beach that had been constructed at the far end of the room. He paddled back to them. He plumped himself down on a towel next to the Fetcher, which he had buried up to its neck in the sand.

'Oh, there's nothing like it . . . I think it's the sea air I notice most. So clear. So pure. You can almost drink it.' He inhaled deeply several times.

'Edward,' said Executive. 'Dreamer thinks you should be getting on with more serious things.'

'Oh, does it? I suppose it can't tell me to my face. Well, tell Dreamer I can do what I damn well like. It's *my* Environment. Hey. Nobody move.' He rested a camera on an upturned bucket and set the timer. 'I want to get a picture of us all together.' He scampered back and lay between the two monitors with an arm round each and an inane seaside grin on his face. It snapped the moment for posterity. 'Anyone fancy a whelk?' No one did. He popped one in his mouth and opened another can of light ale. Dusting the sand from his doorstep-sized holiday fiction, he settled into chapter 58. Captain Davenport had just eluded capture by the KGB at the shattered funfair in war-torn Beirut and was escaping with the fabulous, slinky Sukie into the sewers. The intercom buzzed into Edward's reverie.

'Yes,' he said testily.

'Mr Wilson, sir?'

'Wellinterruptedsecretary-personYourstarterforten NoconferringQuestionone:Whatdoyouwant?'

'Sir Desmond Riley to see you, sir.'

'– is the correct answer! And you have won a fabulous, bubbling bathful of low-calorie yoghurt.'

Sir Desmond paddled in, his grey suit trousers rolled up over his knees. Edward dug the Fetcher out with a spade.

'Fetcher, fizzy drinks all round, but *none* for Dreamer.'

The Fetcher whizzed off to the picnic hamper as Sir Desmond arrived at the beach.

'Hallo, Edward. Is everything all right?'

Edward shifted uneasily in the sand and looked about. 'Why? Shouldn't it be? Something wrong?'

'No,' said Sir Desmond nonchalantly, easing his bulk on to the sand.

'That's easy for *you* to say.' Edward laughed maniacally. 'Stick of rock, Des?' He thrust a pink baton of the stuff at him. 'It's got Room one thousand and one written all the way through it. Or would you fancy a whelk?'

The Fetcher whirred back. 'Fizzy drinks! Fizzy drinks!' it announced.

Sir Desmond eyed it questioningly. 'Fizzy drinks?'

'Fizzy drinks, fizzy drinks, fizzy drinks!' sang Edward.

'Fizzy drinks all round, but *none* for Dreamer,' repeated the Fetcher.

'*None* for Dreamer? *None* for Dreamer?' said Edward in mock amazement. 'What's Dreamer done wrong? Nothing. Nothing. Dreamer not friends with Edward? No . . . Just because it keeps asking me questions doesn't mean to say that it can't have a fizzy drink if it wants one. None for Dreamer, really. Fetcher, where are your manners?' He looked over to Sir Desmond. 'Huh. These Fetchers. *None* for Dreamer! Who could have told the Fetcher none for Dreamer? Certainly not *me*.'

Sir Desmond surveyed the scene. The four inches of water, the little boats, the high-diving board, the Punch and Judy stall . . . Edward was standing over him and glaring down.

'Well, Sir Desmond, we'll let you know. Don't call us. Nice ideas you have, but not good enough for the Environment of tomorrow. Price satisfaction guarantee technology is what we're after.' He pushed an empty can of Retro Lager into Sir Desmond's hand. 'Come again another day. Knock three times on the ceiling if you want me.'

Sir Desmond dusted off the sand and splashed his way back to the door. When he turned his face it was full of pity. Edward's was full of whelks.

'Goodbye,' he said. He stepped over the sandbags and closed the door.

The secretary looked up from biting her fingernails.

'How is he?' she inquired.

'Mad as a hatter. All the signs . . . manic-depressive cycles, paranoia, megalomania, hysteria, delusions . . . Funny what power does to a man.'

The intercom buzzed.

'Secretary-person! Is he here yet?'

The secretary threw a startled, questioning look to Sir Desmond, who shrugged.

'No, sir.'

Edward snorted. 'He's with the Czarina, isn't he? Dirty little priest. Roll on Lenin, that's what I say. Get it over with. *Meine Geduld ist zu Ende. Capito?*'

Transmission ceased. The elderly knight and the care-worn secretary exchanged despondent looks and shook their heads.

'Did he tell you about his creative employment scheme?' asked the secretary. Sir Desmond's heart sank. 'He wants to dig four thousand holes in Blackburn, Lancashire.'

The intercom buzzed again.

'Secretary-person, I'd like to teach the world to sing in perfect harmony.'

'Yes, Mr Wilson, sir.'

'How much can I reasonably charge them, on an hourly basis?'

'I'm afraid that's one for Executive, sir.'

Sir Desmond watched Edward on the monitor. Dreamer was back into full swing.

'Better get a medical team on standby. What company is he with?'

'Red Shield.'

'Good. Better safe than sorry.'

6

HAPPINESS IS WORK

Sophie and Charles were lying on the beach recovering from the night before. The Solomon Islanders certainly knew how to put on a good night's entertainment. The discos that lined the eight miles of hotel frontage of their resort were among the most popular in the whole Melanesian Archipelago, and quite unspoilt by comparison with the rest of the Western Pacific. Charles had excelled himself and he had been justly proud of his dancing. Thanks to his hospital treatment his legs were totally impervious to the effects of alcohol. He could now go beyond his normal limits of leglessness and stay upright and active when his mental faculties had long been rendered supine.

Sophie had gone to bed early with a bottle of After Sun. She was determined to get the tan that had eluded her on all previous holidays. No amount of care seemed to make any difference. From salmon pink, she went cerise, then vermilion. She had awoken that morning, thrilled to find herself coated with the walnut veneer she had always dreamed of, then watched the tan go down the plughole of the shower. She was back to virgin white.

Charles was sleeping off the night before. Memories of the night's revelries filtered down through his muddy cerebrum. He turned lazily and squinted at Sophie's pale slenderness. No, it couldn't have been Sophie ... But there had to be some explanation for that mixture of pride and shame that he was feeling. Otherwise how could everything feel so, well ... post-coital? He turned on to his other side and scanned the beach for a clue. There were plenty of available-looking women around, some of them definitely deserving of the Dartmouth charm, but none of them rang any bells. And he did wake up in the right bed this morning even if he didn't remember how he got there. Maybe he had been a good boy, after all.

Sophie was also wondering how Charles had got into the right bed when he came back to the hotel room at about four that morning, his legs striding with purpose, his upper half fast asleep and swaying precariously. She would wait for a voluntary confession before condemning him. She watched the news on the portable. Although a hardened professional, the news still excited her. It was the mark of a good career mole to remain uncynical about the machinations of the department. She was, however, deeply cynical about Charles' missing hours. She summoned the courage.

'Charles? Last night . . . What did you do after I left you at the Surf 'n' Sun Disco?'

'God, have I been asleep? There's one thing you must *never* do is fall asleep drunk in the sun. You must keep drinking. What was that you said?' He forced a puppy-dog innocence into his red-rimmed eyes with all the obstinacy he could muster. He looked like a leprotic hyena, but it was enough to melt Sophie.

'I wanted to know how my tan was coming on,' she said limply.

'It's coming off. I told you not to trust that suntan stuff. Look at the label: "Store in a cool, dry place, away from direct sunlight".' Charles pretended to go back to sleep.

'Hi,' drawled the newsreader on the portable. 'The main stories again. Seventy-three per cent say no to single-sex lavatories, and that's official. The latest opinion poll shows it's thumbs down for the old-fashioned Ladies and Gents. The Environment's new megaloos will incorporate the very latest in fashion and style, with sports facilities, hairdressing, sunbeds, saunas, restaurants and singles bars. They'll be with us soon. And now the Megamarkets: the latest addition to the line-up looks set to become quite a hit. It's called BabyWorld, but that's all we can tell you for now. Pop along and see for yourself. After the break: the scandal of the growing yoghurt swamp. Stay with us for more of the news *you* want to hear . . .'

Charles' radiophone buzzed. Sophie snatched the receiver, hoping to catch whatever woman Charles might have given his number to at the Surf 'n' Sun. It was Sir Desmond Riley.

'Ah, Sophie. Hallo. I thought I'd ring you to er – How's the Solomon Islands?'

'I'll show you.' She held up the phone.

'Mmmm. Yes. Must be very hot. Good grief. Everyone's topless. Turn it round again. Is that Charles?'

'Hi, Sir Desmond.'

'Put some clothes on, man. Well, how are you two getting on? Point the phone up at your face, Sophie. I can't talk to you like that. That's better. Well. You seem to be enjoying yourselves. Why not come home the slow way? I've managed to get you two executive tickets on the *Princess* from New York. Gets in at Southampton in five days.'

Charles was quick to agree.

'Any news about Edward?' asked Sophie.

'Oh, Edward. He's turned up again. Sends you his love. Got a new job, you know.'

'Really?' said Charles insouciantly.

'Yes. He's *mad* about it. See you when it's all over. Goodbye.'

'When what's all over, Charles?'

'The holiday, Soph.'

'Well, it's nice to know Edward's happy at work.'

Without Charles to help him with the Mainframe, Sir Desmond had increased the surveillance of Edward. He had managed to smuggle television cameras and a microphone into the room and watched him on the telephone whenever he had a spare moment. The secretary was hooked into the same line so that they could discuss developments.

Things had taken a disturbing turn. Edward had risen early, cancelled the war with Russia, and was calmly organizing business with Executive. There had been no tantrums and no acts of violence on the Fetcher. In one hour Edward had reversed every one of his previous orders. It was just as well Executive had stopped carrying them out, anyway, after the yoghurt fiasco and the disastrous Mark 7 Fetcher. The tension was getting to Sir Desmond, who found that a keyboard is a poor substitute for a pencil when you need something to chew.

'Executive,' said Edward breezily. 'Do you have the dairy production forecasts?' Executive displayed them. 'Mmm. What time is the first delegation due?'

'Two o'clock.'

'Right. Get me the breakdown of total energy requirements for nineteen ninety-five and order them against a background of available short- and long-term resources . . . This is a matter of some considerable importance, as you no doubt appreciate, Executive. Now, about the new urban housing scheme. We need something to fulfil the requirements as indicated by your analysis of the most recent polls. I wonder what Dreamer has to offer us on that one . . .?'

Sir Desmond noticed Edward give a shifty glance at Dreamer.

'Executive . . .? Is Dreamer non-operational at the moment?'

'Edward, surely you remember. You told Dreamer never to speak to you again. That was yesterday.'

'Did I? Fancy that. Ha, ha, ha. Well, I'm sure Dreamer understands. That was yesterday. Things were different then. I may have said something silly. We often say things we don't mean, don't we? I wasn't very well earlier. You must have noticed. That's why I was doing all that screaming and shouting. But I'm in control now.' There was a faint tremulo creeping into Edward's voice.

'Here we go,' said Sir Desmond.

'Total and absolute power is a serious business,' asserted Edward, leaning back in the sensible new chair that replaced the throne from yesterday. 'We can't have Dreamer sulking, now, can we?'

'It's no use, Edward. Dreamer says you're mad.'

Edward leant his elbows on his new, sensible desk and glowered menacingly into Executive's monitor. 'Mad, am I? I? Mad? I, who have governed the Environment quite sensibly all day? Mad?' The fury abated and Edward sank back into his managerial posture. 'No matter. Show me the apiary production figures, Executive.'

Executive displayed a world map dotted with statistics and graphs.

'Mmmm. Production is down in The Gambia. Very interesting. Isn't it, *Dreamer*?'

Sir Desmond could see a flicker of desperation in Edward's furtive peek at Dreamer's blank monitor.

'It is interesting to me, Dreamer, and therefore it is interesting to you. I and the Environment are one. *L'Environnement, c'est moi*. Together we shall build a land of milk and honey. What do you think of that, Dreamer? Oh, sorry. Forgot. You can't think, can you? HOW CAN I RUN THE ENVIRONMENT IF YOU DON'T THINK?' A hiatus of boggling gripped him. He summoned his last sliver of certainty. 'But I *am* running the Environment. I *am*.'

He turned to face whatever challenge might come from other sources in the room. The Fetcher was buried under the sand in a far corner and no longer disturbed him. The room had been swept of any remaining trace of insanity. Except—

'Executive. There are cameras in this room. People are watching me.'

Sir Desmond let his face fall into his hands. Those

cameras had taken hours of stealth in the night to install. They had been disguised in a variety of forms. There was a scarecrow, a lampstand, a replica of the *Good Burghers of Calais*, a clump of bushes and an eye-level grill. In horror Sir Desmond and the secretary watched the diminishing coverage as Edward wreaked an orgy of demolition.

This left only audio surveillance. One microphone disguised as a golf ball on a tee sat in the middle of the carpet. They heard Edward stride to the window, open it, stride back to his sensible managing director's cupboard and select a club. He strode back, lined up, coiled and released. *Thwack! Whizzzzzzzzzzz* . . . THUMP. Silence.

'Now what do we do?' said Sir Desmond.

Edward needed to impress the two o'clock delegation. They had to see the office of a man in control of things. He laid a steady finger on the intercom button.

'Secretary-person, I want more sensible office equipment. You know the sort of thing . . . Desks, swivel chairs, anglepoise lamps, ionizers, wall-charts, filing cabinets, *that* sort of thing. Deliver it immediately, would you? Executive will have it sent to you.'

'Can you hear me?' said Sir Desmond from the bottom drawer to the secretary at the top. 'I can't see a thing.'

'Hang on, I'm coming down.' She edged her drawer out and climbed down behind it into the drawer below, carefully closing A–D above her. She repeated the operation until joining Sir Desmond in V–Z.

'Move up, Sir Desmond. I'll take a look at the front.'

Although it was an unusually large filing cabinet, one to satisfy a bureaucratic megalomaniac, movement required painful contortion and a level of unprecedented intimacy between its occupants.

'Ah,' said the secretary. 'I can see what's in the way. The label at the front of the drawer is covering the eyehole.'

'Well, reach out and remove it.'

'Right. Grasp my leg firmly and push. We need to open the drawer.'

With both hands encircling her thigh, he pushed gently. 'All in the cause of duty,' sighed Sir Desmond. 'How's that?'

'Mmm. Fine. Just a bit further.' Sir Desmond's hands slid further along the warm nylon. 'For goodness sake, don't lose your grip, Sir Desmond.'

Sir Desmond was remembering those happy powercut nights during the Difficulties. He and his wife Beryl had produced three children under similar conditions of darkness and confinement and named them after the union leaders that had unwittingly caused their conception. He was certainly losing his grip. He regained it and pushed her leg. She snaked her hand out and slipped the label from its housing.

'Got it.' He pulled her leg back sharply. 'Agh. My hand. You've shut the drawer on it! Open the drawer!'

Edward was relieved to see that the new office equipment was friendly. There was even a filing cabinet waving at him.

'I think I'll go and have a chat with it,' he said.

'Oooh, oooh, oooh!' said the secretary. Sir Desmond took this to be a signal to continue fondling her leg. Edward had nearly reached the cabinet when quick thinking from Executive saved the day.

'Edward . . .?'

'Not now, Executive. I'm talking to a filing cabinet.'

'Edward. *Dreamer* wants to talk to you.'

Edward scrambled back to Dreamer's monitor. 'So you've decided to stop sulking, have you?'

'Sorry,' said Executive. 'My mistake. It must have changed its mind.'

Edward crushed the intercom button. There was a deafening buzz in V–Z next to Sir Desmond's ear. He suffered a violent spasm of shock, which was transmitted directly to the secretary via the fleshier regions of her upper thigh. She shrieked and wriggled free, flailing like a salmon with a pressing engagement upstream and clambered over Sir Desmond towards the intercom. Sir Desmond had no idea she had had the forethought to install it. After knocking his head on the bottom of P–U he had little idea of anything. She hit the talk button.

'Yes, Mr Wilson, sir,' she whispered urgently.

'Secretary-person, why are you whispering?'

'Sore throat.'

'What's going on?' wailed Sir Desmond. She covered the intercom with one hand and Sir Desmond's mouth with the other.

'He's got to think we're still in reception.'

'Secretary-person, there's a filing cabinet in here. It's been waving at me,' blared the intercom.

'It's one of your fans.'

'Why's it stopped, then?'

The secretary braced herself against Sir Desmond's stomach and pushed. The drawer opened. 'Wave,' she hissed. Sir Desmond waved lamely.

'It's all right,' said the intercom. 'It's waving again. Now, the delegation. Have they arrived?'

'Yes.'

'Good, Send them in.'

'Certainly Mr Wilson, sir.'

'How are we going to do that?' hissed Sir Desmond. 'We can't open the door from here.'

'There's no delegation either. What's he doing?'

The portly knight squinted through the hole. Edward was greeting a group of visitors, shaking hands and offering them sensible chairs to sit on. The visitors were silent and invisible. Edward was speaking in his smoothest, most directorial manner.

'Good. Good. That's encouraging. What do you think, Watkins? Mmmmmm . . . Mmm! Aha. Well, that's all very well, Cartwright, but will there be enough Bounty bars for everyone?'

'What can be going on inside that poor head of his?' mused Sir Desmond.

Everything was going on inside that poor head of his. Edward had withdrawn to an interior world, one which *he* was in charge of. Total power and freedom of choice had not only gone to his head, they had climbed in and blocked the exit.

The delegation of dedicated experts was reporting its researches into that old chestnut, Utopia. He had sent them off to make a comparative study of all the known plans for Paradise, the Promised Land, Xanadu and Erewhon. He was chasing the very chimeric vision that Sir Desmond had seen once and was beginning to think would never be realized. Edward was in Cloud Cuckoo Land and was ruling it wisely and well.

'Well, Smith?'

Smith's voice echoed through swathes of mist. 'Well, sir. Kublai Khan's plans are quite specific in terms of physical outline, but –'

'Smith, stop echoing and come closer.'

Smith came closer and stopped echoing. 'Certainly, sir.'

Sir Desmond peered in disbelief at the madman who ranted into thin air. 'Not much longer, I should think,' he murmured.

Inside Edward's crazed psyche, the discussion was ranging beyond the bounds of its own wayward logic.

'That's it!' he exclaimed. 'I've got it! We'll build a leisure dome over the whole Environment. A geodesic leisure dome. Then we'll switch off all gravity in the world.'

'But . . .' Smith's objection was overruled.

'I know what you're going to say. But, don't you see? With the dome to stop the children from floating off into outer space, we won't need to waste valuable energy resources on gravitational pull. It would be so beautiful.'

'But . . .' It was too late. Thought and deed were inseparable, and the dream had already realized itself. Edward and his delegation were floating weightlessly above the Environment, swimming lazily in a clear, windless atmosphere, one which was maintained at room temperature by a device Edward was yet to invent.

An ideal couple of young marrieds drifted past blissfully. 'Hallo!' they called.

'Isn't it marvellous,' said the man, 'now that Edward Wilson's made everything perfect . . .'

'Yes,' swooned the woman. 'I *love* him.'

A volunteer squad of the Difficult Day police levitated into a tight cordon around Edward. The delegation managed to swim away and were eating a little way off at Skylab burger bar. The chief constable drew his truncheon, tapped it on his riot shield and conducted the circle of volunteers, who sang:

'It won't work, sonny. You can't defy the laws of gravity and get away with it. You're nicked.'

As one, the young marrieds and the delegates sang back: 'Can't you?' And promptly fell earthwards.

'You've killed them!' protested Edward. 'I could cut your telephone off for that!'

The volunteers looked down at the small cards they held in their hands and with a nod from the truncheon, they chorused: 'Edward Wilson. You are under arrest. You are not obliged to say anything, but anything you do say we hold the recording rights to. Any royalties that may accrue may be deemed the property of the . . .'

'Go away!' cried Edward. 'Don't come near me! I demand an agent!'

An intercom button bobbed uncertainly into Edward's field of vision. He pressed it.

'Secretary-person!' roared the intercom in V–Z. 'Tell these policemen to . . . Tell them to . . .'

'What the hell's he raving about?' wondered Sir Desmond, who could only hear one half of the drama.

Edward and the volunteer police proceeded in an earthly direction and hit the ground at terminal velocity. For

Edward, understandably, everything went black. Sir Desmond watched him fall over on to the big, big carpet, where he lay unconscious.

The nightmare continued unabated. Edward was now in a stone cellar. Bright lights shone savagely into his face.

'I won't talk! I won't talk!' he protested.

'So. You won't talk,' concluded a cruel voice behind the lights.

'What do you want me to talk *about*?'

'Right. You asked for this, you intransigent little bastard. Harry! He's all yours.'

Steel-tipped boots scraped across bare stone. A heavy lock turned and an iron door opened boomingly. More boots ground heavily across the flagstones. Edward pleaded for mercy.

'Hallo. Do you mind if I sit down?' said Harry. 'Gosh. This room's in a mess, isn't it? Now, I've got a few questions for you and I want honest answers.' An opinion board flashed into view. Harry adjusted one of the lights to display his own sweet smile. He pressed an intercom button.

'Tea for two, please.' 'Tea for Two' wafted from a tannoy. Harry pressed again. 'Er . . . Could you make that "Just a Song at Twilight"?' 'Just a Song at Twilight' came caressingly into the dank air. 'Now, Edward. What's your view of the Environment?'

'Well, I think –'

'Ah-ah-ah. Is it: A, Quite nice; B, Fun; C, Exciting; D, Miraculous; or E, Super?'

'The Environment is the enemy of free will.'

'Mmm. Is free will: A, Doing your own thing; B, Choice; or C, The exercise of volition?'

'I don't know.'

'Is that because: A, –'

'Oh. Just stop. It's A. A!'

'There,' soothed Harry. 'I'm sure you've made the right choice.'

'No. There's something missing . . .'

'Try religion. The choice is infinite and probably eternal. There's High Church, Low Church, Methodist, Baptist, Seventh Day Adventism, Mormonism – that one's quite good for getting out and meeting people – then there's all the Eastern religions, and Greek Orthodox, which is sort of halfway between East and West, lots of lovely icons and triptychs. Judaism is supposed to be quite nice, though you might find the initiation a bit inconvenient, if you see what I mean. Islam. That has the advantage of polygamy, if that's your cup of tea, as with Mormonism. Actually, you can't drink tea as a Mormon, or coffee, or alcohol, and you mustn't smoke. With Islam, it's just alcohol you can't touch. All in all, you might find that a bit restricting – though the clothing can be quite exotic. I know. Let's go to the Multidenominational Church of St Elsewhere.'

Harry opened a door behind Edward. It led to a gallery looking down on a vast congregation in a brightly lit cathedral of white concrete. The priest was down among the throng with a microphone, beaming at his flock. Some were facing Mecca, some were kneeling, some were sitting cross-legged on rush matting and others were holding hands in a circle.

The priest was in mid-sermon. '. . . and this parable can serve to tell us many things. Perhaps it could mean that truly there was a miracle. Or perhaps it might merely serve as a metaphor for many things: the all-pervading flow of Karma, Godhead, the love of Christ, the wisdom of Mohammed, or the oneness and harmony of Man, Woman and Nature. Or is it just, as some scholars have postulated, a spurious part of the text, thought by many to have been introduced in the third century by Pope Hormisdas, his wife, or his boyfriend? The choice, as a believer, is yours . . .'

The priest stepped into a Perspex lift, which carried him majestically to an organ loft crammed with keyboards, synthesizers, rhythm machines, cables and amplifiers.

'Now, let us all hold hands, or prostrate ourselves, or

just stand still and look serious for hymn number four hundred and thirty-seven, omitting the somewhat contentious verses four and six, unless of course you feel strongly about keeping them in. Ahem. "Welcome To My House, O Lord, Or Would You Prefer To Go Somewhere Else?"'

He kissed a touch-sensitive panel and an almighty torrent of decibels crashed into the congregation in the opening salvo of solid disco.

Edward felt a powerful urge to run. Harry had disappeared. The back wall of the gallery was lined with doors. He chose one at random and ran along a winding series of corridors, stairways and anterooms into a great, oak-panelled courtroom. Eyes fixed him in the doorway. The judge was a man who had played Franz Kafka's father in a recent television comedy series. The jury applauded to the command of a studio floor-manager. They were cheering Edward. A red light flashed on a camera that wheeled round to the judge. He tapped his gavel and invited Edward to come on down into the dock. The jury cheered. 'Silence in court!' roared the judge. 'Edward Wilson, you are charged that on diverse occasions you said things knowingly, or reckless as to their being, contrary to public opinion. And we'll have the first prosecution witness after this.'

On a giant monitor behind the bench burst an abstract conflagration of colour. Disco-funk belted from concealed speakers.

'Worried you're not getting enough disco news?' enquired a gravelly black voice. 'Well, you won't ever again with new Discaid. Fits snug as a bug in your lug, tells you what's on, where to go, who to meet, plus all those funky sounds. Like *uh*! and *ah*! Discaid. The greatest aid of the decade.'

The judge struck his gavel and whirled to face the camera. 'Welcome back. I call the first witness.'

The witness *dibidibidibied* towards the witness box, and nearly got there.

'May the witness give its evidence from the floor?' asked the prosecution.

'Certainly,' assured the judge cheerily. 'As Edward's Fetcher, tell us how it all started.'

'It all started when he bought me,' squeaked the Fetcher in infantile tones of aggrievement. The jury *aaahed* in sympathy. A camera closed in on a middle-aged woman dabbing tears from her eye with a lilac tissue from a box of Weepeaze. 'He didn't really *choose* me.' Another took a stern reaction-shot of the judge. 'He just pointed in my direction *without even looking*, and said: "OK. That one."' The jury murmured disapproval. 'I think it all must go back to his childhood.'

'I call Edward's childhood!' commanded the judge.

'Edward's childhood! Edward's childhood!' echoed the corridor telegraph.

On the giant monitor appeared the hallway of Edward's suburban home in 1971. He felt a lump form in his throat. He had forgotten how drab the world was then. His mother was pulling on a fake-fur coat over a short Crimplene dress. The jury guffawed at her high white boots with stacked heels. Edward turned to the jury in impotent rage. But their faces had changed to show untrammelled pity. Turning back to the monitor, he saw himself at the age of four in short grey trousers, a thick pullover and a gabardine mac. He was sitting on the stairs, his head in his hands. Mittens dangled from elastic cords in his sleeves. He was crying.

'But I don't want to go, Mummy!'

The adult Edward was close to tears himself. A hot surge of self-pity welled up inside him. How small he was then. How big the house. How cruel the world.

'But we *must* go, Edward,' said the young mother with tired sternness. 'It's the January sale.' She pulled his little hand and led him into the frosty air.

The scene cut to the local department store. The jury hooted at its old-fashioned paltriness. How stupidly unappealing it looked now, even to Edward. Edward Junior was, however, overawed. Too short to see his mother on the other side of the counter where she was fighting over a stiff white brassiere with another eager shopper, he had begun to panic. His eyes looked as if they were about to burst. Low camera-angles gave emphasis to his vulnerability. Great legs in wide flares swished past him on the grubby linoleum. Young Edward came dramatically into close-up as the slow, complex contortions that precede a tantrum aligned themselves on his face.

'Mummy! Mummy! I've lost my mummy!' he cried. 'I'm in my formative years. This could be a traumatic experience!'

'Well, Edward?' enquired the judge. 'How are you feeling? More guilty?'

'I don't know,' admitted Edward. 'What do you think?'

'Who am I to judge?' snorted the judge. 'Hardly the point. Any other witnesses?'

The prosecution read from a list on his monitor. 'There's his fridge, his radio, his television, a phone box, the Totally Reverend and Wholly Holy Dr Calvin—'

'No,' interrupted the judge wearily. 'I've heard enough. Members of the jury, I'd like a word with you, after this.'

The giant monitor became a bright modern scene outside one of the Megamarkets. Two young women of the probably-married-but-still-very-alluring category were laughing merrily.

'Oh, Jane,' said the tall blonde one admiringly. 'You're so popular. Everyone smiles when they see you. Why?'

'That's *my* secret,' replied the shorter redhead coyly. 'But I'll tell *you*. I've had a Fix 'n' Smile.'

'Fix 'n' Smile?'

'Yes. Fix 'n' Smile. A simple, safe operation that leaves you with a permanent grin, however low you feel.'

The blonde beamed ecstatically. 'That's great! I'll get one tomorrow!'

'I can see it's cheered you up already!'

Together they faced the camera and grinned. 'Fix 'n' Smile!' they chanted, and disappeared.

'Hi, and welcome back,' said the judge. 'Now then, jury. It's verdict time. Fingers on the buzzers, no conferring. Are you ready? Go!'

The jury members pressed frantically. The judge peered at the instant read-out on his private monitor.

'And seventy-three per cent find the defendant guilty.'

Seventy-three per cent of the jury cheered.

'Well . . .' teased the judge. 'That's not what I've got written on my card . . .' He cupped his hand to his earpiece and frowned. 'Hang on. Yes . . . Yes. We *can* allow that. So, guilty by seventy-three per cent is the correct verdict!' He held up his hands to subdue the cheers. 'But I'll have to record an open verdict and hand the matter over to the experts. Let them in, please.'

The doors burst open behind Edward as a horde of men and women with portable cassette recorders and cameras lunged towards him. Trapped in the dock, he thrashed vainly against them to escape as flashguns popped and motor drives whirred.

'Mr Wilson, could you answer a few questions?'

'Mr Wilson, do you feel it was a fair trial?'

'Mr Wilson, can you tell us how you feel about the verdict?'

'Mr Wilson!'

'Mr Wilson!'

The gavel crashed them into silence. The judge cleared his throat. 'Now. Can we have a starting price for this unique personal interest story? Who can offer me fifty thousand?'

'Fifty-two!'

'Fifty-five!'

'Sixty!'

'I wonder when he's going to come round?' said Sir Desmond. 'He hasn't moved for half an hour.'

'It's too quiet, Sir Desmond. I don't like it.'

'Ah. He's stirring.'

Lying flat on his back, Edward was climbing a rope ladder to a helicopter that had flown into court to rescue him.

'Let go of my legs!' he shouted. He pulled himself unsteadily to his feet and blinked. The interior of the helicopter was oddly familiar. He teetered towards the filing cabinet.

Sir Desmond braced himself for the moment of truth. 'Softly the light is dawning upon his fevered brow,' he breathed.

Edward heaved open the bottom drawer. 'Sir Desmond!'

'Hallo, Edward.'

'What are you doing inside this filing cabinet?'

'Well, I'm—'

'You've got to help me, Sir Desmond.'

'How?'

'Get me out of here!'

'I can't. You're in charge of the Environment.'

'Can't you get someone else to do it?'

'Who?'

'I don't know. Anybody. Someone like Sophie. *I* don't care.'

Sir Desmond exhaled heavily. 'There, there, Edward.'

'You did very well, Edward,' soothed the secretary from the back of the drawer. 'Didn't he, Dreamer?'

Dreamer hummed brightly back into life. 'Congratulations, Edward. It's all over now.'

'It's all over now, Charles,' sighed Sophie as they approached Passport Control at Southampton.

'The Environment welcomes you,' said the security turnstile. 'Please place your thumbs on the pads.'

'What's this for, Charles?'

'Oh, nothing to worry about, Soph. It's a blood-test. A little needle shoots up and – ow!'

'The results will be displayed in the Quarantine Lounge in ten minutes,' announced the turnstile as it let them through.

'Did we buy all our duty-free, Soph?'

'I don't think we got the full quota of perfume.'

'Sneak through. They won't notice. Come on.'

Sir Desmond met Charles in the lobby.

'Sir Desmond!'

'Hallo, Charles. Where's Sophie?'

'She got caught with not enough perfume. She's had to go and get some more. I warned her. Women, eh?'

'I've got some news. It's all over with Wilson.'

'Oh, that's great. Here comes Sophie. Look, don't mention her tan. She's very upset.'

She flung her arms around Sir Desmond's tubby neck. 'Desipoohs!'

'Ah,' he blushed. 'My word, tan's er . . . Great. Well, in places anyway. Good holiday?'

'Mmmmmmmmmm!' said the happy couple.

A gentle *bing-bong* radiated through the musak.

'That'll be the blood-test announcement,' gloated Charles. 'There's always some poor idiot who's caught something really embarrassing.'

'WILL CHARLES DARTMOUTH PLEASE REPORT TO THE QUARANTINE LOUNGE. PLEASE DO NOT TALK TO ANYONE ON THE WAY,'

announced the Tannoy.

Sir Desmond and Sophie passed a pensive journey on the shuttle service to London. Sophie didn't begin to perk up until the train was gliding past the new Woking Megamarket.

'Any news of Edward, Sir Desmond?'

'What? Oh, Wilson. No. Haven't seen him for weeks. I expect he's at home.'

'I can't wait to tell him my news.'

'Yes.'

'You will come to our party, won't you?'

'Delighted.'

'We'll be sending out the invitations as soon as Charles gets out of quarantine.'

'Yes. Bad luck, that.'

'I know. We've only been married two days.'

At Surbiton, Sophie hopped off and waved goodbye to Sir Desmond. The doors hissed shut and the train moved on.

'Goodbye . . . Goodbye . . . That's all I seem to be saying these days,' sighed Sir Desmond.

One December afternoon in 1994 a Skysmile helicopter was making its regular sweep over Hyde Park. It was a cold day for waving, and a thin layer of snow had driven the wary into the warmth of the Megamarket. The scanner picked out a non-waver sitting alone on a park bench overlooking the Serpentine. The Mainframe diagnosed illness in the family and reported low consuming levels in recent months.

'What a mizzog,' jeered the pilot. Mainframe recommended ground support. The pilot picked up his receiver.

'Hallo, Eddie. Come in, Eddie. This is Skysmile. Got one for you in Sector A. Two hundred yards dead ahead. Husband dangerously ill or something.'

Eddie acknowledged, took a swig of meths, coughed, spat, shoved a hand into the pocket of his filthy overcoat, rubbed his chin with the other and shuffled off to Sector A.

Sophie was staring gloomily across the Serpentine when a dirty brown object sat down next to her and coughed disgustingly.

'Hallo, darlin'. Cold, innit? Still. Christmas coming. Got any money?'

'Go away.'

'Wossup, me ol' china? – *Sophie!*'

'*Edward!* Why are you dressed as a tramp?'

'I *am* one. Well, one day a week I am, anyway. It's a good job. Well, there's no such thing as a job nowadays, is there? It's a good professional pastime. Cheers people up.'

They both gazed across the Serpentine, unable to meet each other's eye.

'I heard you got married,' said Edward flatly.

'Yes.'

'Congratulations.'

Edward looked down at his filthy, battered shoes.

'Who to? Anyone I know?'

'Charles Dartmouth.'

'Oh.'

'Are you surprised?'

'Not really. I suppose you're made for each other.'

'He's in quarantine and he won't tell me what it is.'

'It's a type of isolation, to stop the spreading of dis—'

'I know what *quarantine* is. I don't know what – oh, never mind.'

'Sorry. I thought you meant . . .'

'I know what you meant.' They sat in uncomfortable silence for a full minute.

'Still, apart from all that, you seem well . . .'

'Yes. What have you been up to?'

'Oh. This and that. I gave Sir Desmond a message to give to you.'

'Did you?'

'Yes. I'm surprised you never got it. I was running the Environment for a while, you know. I'm surprised you never found out.'

'Oh, I never do much moling these days.'

It struck Edward that Sophie had changed in some ill-defined way.

'What happened?' she asked, fiddling with the clasp of her handbag.

'Oh, I had absolute power. But I blew it. Didn't know what I wanted, really. I wasn't up to it. I'm hardly an expert, am I? Besides, the Environment's wonderful enough as it is. And it's getting better and better. I thought I could change things, but it doesn't need anyone to run it.'

The bitter wind was squeezing water from Edward's eyes. They seemed to have so much in common once, but he couldn't for the life of him remember what it was.

'Have you done your Christmas shopping yet?' asked Sophie, admiring her new winter boots.

'Oh, ages ago. There's a fabulous range in Santa Claus' Grotto at the Megamarket. And such good value.'

'I suppose I really ought to get going and do some shopping now,' said Sophie, rising. They walked through the snow, snugly protected from the December wind by the latest in winter fashion. From a distance they resembled two tiny models in a snowstorm paperweight.

'Well,' said Edward. 'I'd better get back to my Fetcher. It gets terribly worried if I'm out for too long.'

'I'll invite you to our party when Charles gets out of quarantine.'

'Yes. We must meet again.'

'Yes, we must.'

On the day of Charles' release, Sir Desmond was paying a last visit to his office to collect some personal possessions. The workmen were stripping the building of all fixtures and fittings. He sat down in his office chair and gazed solemnly and for the last time into his Mainframe monitor. He pressed the intercom button.

'Secretary-person.'

'Yes, Sir Desmond,' she tinkled.

'Tell the workmen I don't want to be disturbed for a while, will you?'

'Certainly, sir.'

'One last try, for old time's sake,' he sighed.

Tentatively he stabbed at the keys. To his utter surprise he got through. Encouraged, he summoned archives and got through again. He decided to type in one last memo. It ran:

20 December 1994. The Environment is at last all around us. The Department is therefore no longer a necessary part of it, and no longer exists.

It has been a slow climb from the Difficulties to Sellingfield and the Wilson Project, the results of which are being used to set us all on an immutable course. The perfect society has been achieved where, from test-tube to incinerator, everyone will enjoy the freedom of a billion trivial decisions in response to a billion trivial bits of information.

Every decision is crucial because it is the act upon which the Environment depends: useless because it cannot change the Environment in any way. In a world where the colour of wallpaper is more important than the colour of government – a choice which no longer exists and will never be missed. At last the Environment is all around us. Forever.

'Well,' thought Sir Desmond, nodding wistfully, 'someone in the future might be interested to know . . .'

There was a sharp knock on the door and Charles Dartmouth bounced in.

'Ah, Charles. Nice to see you fit and well.'

'Hi, Sir Desmond. I just got out in time for Christmas and now I find I've got to get all my stuff out of here and say goodbye to the old place. Sad in a way.'

'Oh well. At least it gives us all more time to have fun.'

'Can't now,' Charles held up his ring-finger. 'Spliced.'

'Your choice, Charles.'

'Don't remind me. That reminds me. Saw Edward the other day buying a new kitchen. He seems OK now.'

'Yes. He'll be voted Consumer of the Year before long.'

'Sir Desmond, what was actually happening with Edward?'

'The results of the Sellingfield Experiment weren't enough, but now we know—'

'God!' exclaimed Charles. 'Is that the time? I've got to meet Sophie in BabyWorld.'

'Ah. The pitter-patter—'

'I know. Next stop Pensionland. Bye, Sir Desmond.'

Charles turned on his heel and sauntered off.

Sir Desmond returned his eye to the memo shimmering on the screen. He pressed the erase button and turned off the machine.

Charles and Sophie had decided to give each other an extra present for Christmas to celebrate Charles' clean bill of health. Choosing its exact form was proving trickier than they had thought.

The relaxed atmosphere of the BabyWorld Selection Surgery encouraged long and careful consideration. Prospective clients were issued with green surgeons' outfits to instil in them a sense of occasion and create an aura of medical responsibility. Nursery-rhyme musak tripped merrily from the walls to balance the effect with a certain imaginative felicity.

'Oh, I don't know, Charles. What do you think?'

Charles looked up at the screen. 'Well, that one takes after you. It's going to need all of my charm.'

'Would you like to see some others?' asked the gentle Irish matron.

'No, no. Let's see,' pondered Sophie. 'This one's got *my* eyes—'

'My eye*lids*. Hang on. I've forgotten. Is this one a boy or a girl?'

'It's a *girl*.'

'He'd better have my legs, then. And my skin. You burn too easily.'

'All right. Let's see what *she'd* look like with that lot.'

The matron fed in the amendments.

'What about when he's twenty?' asked Charles.

The matron hit the age button.

'Looks a bit effeminate, Soph.'

'It's a *girl*, Charles.'

'Oh. Right. Her eyes are a bit close together, though.'

Charles assumed control of the keyboard.

'Charles, she looks like a locust now. You're not taking this seriously.'

'How can I, with a nose like that?'

He set about creating his own idea of perfect woman and sat back to admire his work. 'That's better,' he leered.

'*Charles.*'

'I'm sorry,' the matron lilted. 'But like that it's going to get very fat later on in life. The computer can juggle the genes but it can't work miracles. How's this?'

'Mmm,' said Sophie. 'Quite nice.'

'Yeah. OK,' conceded Charles. 'Or how about a boy?'

'We've been here for *three and a half hours*.'

'Yeah, but it's so difficult to choose.'

'Why not take home the BabyWorld Mix 'n' Match Disk?' suggested the matron. 'That can be programmed with all your gene combinations, bearing in mind your low sperm-count.'

'Do you mind. I've had a long day.'

'No,' said Sophie. 'I'll have this one.'

'Yeah. That'll do . . . Is this one going to be clever?'

'I've already explained, Mr Dartmouth. It can't work miracles.'

'What d'you mean?'

'Of course, there is the two-way surrogate option . . .'

'Well, Charles?'

'No. I'll buy that.'

'Good.' The matron heaved a sigh of relief. 'We do think

it's important for both of you to be present at the conception, but after that, of course . . . Have a Merry Christmas and a Happy New Year.'

On New Year's Eve, Edward and his Fetcher set out to join the queue for the opening of the January sale at the London Megamarket. The queue stretched from the St Paul's entrance, up Ludgate Hill, Fleet Street and the Strand as far as Trafalgar Square, where the traditional merrymaking was in full swing. The water in the fountains had been especially heated to avoid unpleasant chills and was already full of splashing revellers.

Edward and his Fetcher took their place at the back of the queue and watched the fun. The Tannoy boomed into life.

'Ha, ha, ha. Hallo, and welcome again! We're just five minutes away from nineteen ninety-five, so let's keep the party going, and remember: Keep it safe! Ha-ha. Here's an old one I know you'll just *love*!'

Edward thrilled to the lights and the jolly music that filled the square.

'I hope there's some bargains left by the time we get there, Fetcher, don't you?'

'Oooh yes!' trilled the Fetcher.

'Still, we get all the fun of the square at this end. It looks better than ever. The video screen's enormous.'

An eager bargain-hunter turned his wide eyes to Edward. 'Yeah. It's thirty feet wider than last year. They had to knock the National Gallery down to get it in.'

Edward gasped.

Overhead a Skysmile helicopter thundered into view. Edward's feet made convulsive movements. He looked up at the flying spirit of freedom and happiness. He waved and cheered and smiled in an ecstasy of jumping.

'Happy New Year! Happy New Year!' he called in glorious unison with the crowd. When the helicopter had passed over, he returned his attention to the video screen. A presenter was speaking from outside the St Paul's entrance.

'Now, as midnight approaches, viewers all over the Environment are queueing for the fabulous January sales. And here in London is the most envied man in the whole Environment. He's the one at the front of the queue, and he's been here for – how long?'

'Six weeks.'

'And what is it that's so special waiting for you inside the Megamarket?'

'Camping equipment.'

'For that special holiday?'

'No. So I won't be so cold queueing next year.'

'Ha, ha, ha. Well, back to Damian in the studio.'

Edward patted his Fetcher on its domed head. 'You all right, Fetcher?'

'Ooh, yes, Edward. Happy New Year.'

'Aah. And you, Fetcher. Happy New Year.'

The video screen displayed a close-up of Big Ben. The hands had nearly got there.

'Coming up soon after midnight,' bellowed the screen, 'a special announcement from the Megamarkets. That's after this.'

Big Ben gave way to a series of shots of young people enjoying LIFE, the Special Kind of Fizzy Drink. Big Ben reappeared and began its introductory chimes.

Edward's pulse was racing.

'What a year, Fetcher. So much has happened. And next year's going to be even better.'

'We had a lovely Christmas, didn't we Edward?'

'Yes . . . Just you and me. And the television. Where would we be without that?'

The opening verse of 'Auld Lang Syne' burst from the screen. On the twelfth stroke of midnight, a raucous roar from the crowd drowned the music.

The announcer chose his moment as the cacophony

subsided. 'And now that important announcement from the Megamarkets!'

The whole of London waited in tense silence.

'The doors are open. And the prices are ... Yes! Twenty-five per cent down!'

A cheer that surpassed all others erupted into the night air. Edward stood in a blissful dream. Tears of joy trickled down the sides of his nose. It was more than all right. He had won the biggest prize of them all. He loved the Environment.

APPENDIX
THE PRINCIPLES OF ADSPEAK

Adspeak was the unofficial language of the Environment and had been devised to promote the policies of the Environment. In 1994 there was not as yet anyone who used Adspeak as his sole means of communication, either in speech or in writing. The leading articles in *The Times* were written in it, but this was a *tour de force* which could only be carried out by a specialist.

The purpose of Adspeak was to make all but orthodox modes of thought impossible. This was achieved partly by the invention of new words, or by using the same word many times over for many different things, and of course by eliminating many words altogether. To give a simple example: the word *free* proliferated in Adspeak, but could only be used in such statements as 'Buy two and get one free' or 'Admission free'. It could not be used in the sense of 'politically free' or 'intellectually free' since such concepts were considered boring, mad or unfashionable. Quite apart from the suppression of various words, the reduction of vocabulary was an end in itself as a matter of pure aesthetics.

In Adspeak there was no rigidly defined grammatical or semantic battle plan. The language evolved haphazardly through artificial enhancement of the natural processes of assimilation. It was an effective procedure, for it meant that people began speaking Adspeak without realizing that they were doing so, in exactly the same way that a child learns from its parents. To quote a simple example again: since the word *bonanza* was used to describe every single event which conferred gratuitous benefit, whether material or emotional, it soon became unnecessary to use any other word; and since no other word was ever used by the Environment, people soon forgot that there were other words available and plumped for that one. *Bonanza* had passed from being a 'buzz-word' in the eighties, through being a 'byword', past the status of 'watchword' and become a 'megaword' (literally: word with a million uses). To give a demonstration both of its application and of its effect on the use of other words, the following well-known passage from the *Declaration of Independence*:

We hold these truths to be self-evident, that all men are created equal, that they are endowed by their Creator with certain unalienable rights, that among these are life, liberty, and the pursuit of happiness. That to secure these rights, Governments are instituted among men, deriving their just powers from the consent of the governed. That whenever any form of Government becomes destructive of these ends, it is the right of the people to alter or to abolish it, and to institute new government . . .

can be reduced to the simple phrase: 'Bonanza for the People!'

Furthermore, the application of such words to almost every conceivable situation – be it mundane or highly dramatic – had the other main purpose of encouraging people to speak and therefore think in absolutes. This meant that the language retained only black and white words. All grey words were expunged from the language. To give an example: a mediocre film would only be described as either megafantastic or completely turn-offable. By using positive superlatives more often than negative ones to describe aspects of life, good or bad, people viewed even the most miserable disasters as entertaining. One can take as another example a recent headline concerning a fatal railway accident:

COO! RAILBREAK JOCK!
SCOTTISH LOCO GOES LOCO

This maintenance at all times of hyperbole ensured that no serious issues or questions could ever arise.

Another important effect of Adspeak was to make people react emotionally in a hyperbolic but essentially unnatural way. Everything that happened could only be described in terms of the fantastically wonderful or the appallingly awful. Such a process quickly cheapened the experience. The effect created was one of levelling emotion at a high pitch. Missing a train was described in exactly the same terms as the death of a loved one. Both were 'completely tragic'. A person growing up with Adspeak as his sole language would not know of milder ways to describe the former experience and would therefore be unable to distinguish its gravity from that of the latter. All his emotions would be defined and therefore *con*fined by an extremely limited set of adjectives. This would mean that sooner or later his emotions themselves would be entirely reduced to basics.

Finally, the underlying purpose of Adspeak was to encourage the general despising of anything that was ordinary or commonplace. In a world of hyperbole, the mundane was a thing of ridicule and derision. This was again important, in that, should people think about things in terms of the ordinary, there was a danger that they might see the world in too realistic a light. Furthermore, if the Environment had been spoken or thought of as ordinary, then it would have failed to be the totally amazing funpark it was cracked up to be. The highest insult that one could pay to anyone was to accuse them of being 'ordinary'. To describe someone's sex life as 'boring' was heresy. It would have been essential to describe it along the following lines: 'Amazing shock claim of passionless love-merchant – "My nights of sexathons are totally non-existent"!!!'

It is generally believed that Adspeak will become the *lingua franca* for the Environment by the year 2060. That year has already been heralded as 'the most megafantastic wonderyear in the history of creation'.